# THE FOOL

*Dreams, Synchronicities and Miracles in a
Journey to Find One's Real Self*

Dimitrios Papalexis, MCC

BALBOA.
PRESS
A DIVISION OF HAY HOUSE

Edited by
Erisana Sanches Victoriano
Stephen John Hodgins

Balboa Press books may be ordered through booksellers or by contacting:

Balboa Press
A Division of Hay House
1663 Liberty Drive
Bloomington, IN 47403
www.balboapress.com
1-(877) 407-4847

ISBN: 978-1-4525-5590-4 (sc)
ISBN: 978-1-4525-5589-8 (e)

Printed in the United States of America

Balboa Press rev. date: 8/15/2012

"As you move beyond the words and into the essence of this book you will experience your own life transforming as you read."

Gini Grey, author of From Chaos to Calm

*"And you will know the truth, and the truth will set you free."*

*John 8:32*

*To my love Erisana, who is always a challenge and inspiration for me.*

# Contents

# FOREWORD

Getting lost in my work, in the busy overpopulated city life and in my PhD studies of complex theories of language and society seem to have played a role in my moving away from the simple crucial things that life has to offer us. The Fool has played an important role in pushing me back to this direction which I feel to be so relevant if you want to live a fulfilled life. While I traveled through its pages, following Danny's journey, I had the chance to remember so many things I had forgotten, how beautiful it is to have dreams and follow them, the risks we have to take sometimes in life, the synchronicities that chase us every day and so many others...

The Fool also reminds us about the calls we have in our lives, which many times are ignored. By following Danny's adventure, it is possible to see that we are not the only ones to question our calls. After all do calls exist? Are they just our imagination? I believe it is almost impossible to read The Fool and not identify ourselves with it. Have you ever found yourself living a life which would cause jealousy to so many people, but brings unhappiness to you? And when you look around you do see the "ideal life" surrounding you and you do not have a clue why you do not feel the happiest. In a period like that my happiest moments were made by watching cargo trains passing by, going to their secret places. In my imagination, I was inside them going to a faraway place too. I think somehow like Danny, I was also looking for God's nest.

As I have not only been given the grace of reading The Fool, but also of meeting the author professionally and then personally, I can tell that Danny's courage, honesty and determination reflect Dimitrios himself. In addition Dimitrios has had the privilege of experiencing the literal and metaphoric trips that Danny takes during the book. Literally he has lived in three different continents, "tasted" three different cultures and can take the best of these experiences to share with his readers. Metaphorically he has also experienced inner changes which he brilliantly describes in The Fool's pages.

On one hand writing about The Fool differs from everything I have been writing during the last decade of my academic career. On the other hand it feels so at home, because many aspects of Danny's journey reflect my own inner journey which has been so important to help me living a balanced life. I hope everyone who reads this book can enjoy the "journey" as much as I did and take the best of it.

Erisana Sanches Victoriano, PhD

# PREFACE

The idea or, better, intuition to write down this story came unexpectedly one day when I was in the car passing by a beautiful natural landscape in Brazil. In that day, I was looking at the mountains when suddenly I felt some inspiration and started "downloading" in my mind the first chapter of the story. Actually, I had to put some effort to stop "the download" so I could wait until I had the chance to get out of the car and turn on my laptop so I could write it down before I forgot it. I use the word "download" because it was not as if I thought about it and took a logical decision to write a book. It was something much deeper than that, a sudden inspiration to write a story that I started channelling from above. While I kept channelling the story and writing it down, I was also getting excited to know the rest. I knew that the story hid profound messages that could change me and all others who read this book.

In order to reach this point in my life, many important people have helped me become the person I am today. First of all, I would like to thank my significant other, Erisana Sanches Victoriano, from Brazil. She has been not only an amazing partner, but also has always challenged me to be honest with myself and pushed me forward to growth and expansion. She was also the first person to read my book and offer valuable feedback about the story. I also have to express my gratitude to my mother Aristea, my father Constantinos and my sister Vasiliki from Sydney, Australia, for always supporting and loving me unconditionally. I will thank next my friend Dimitris Papadimitriou from Volos, Greece, for believing in me and insisting from the very beginning that I should write a book. Also, I would like to thank my friend Stephen Hodgins from Newcastle, Australia, and Gini Grey from Canada, who both provided me with valuable tips about the book and especially Stephen for helping me with the editing process. Finally, I would like to thank all the people and animals that I have met in my life and are part of my story, physical and spiritual journey.

# Introduction

Danny, a young lawyer from Sydney, Australia, of Greek origin, is married and has two kids. He is pursuing a prominent career as a lawyer for an important law firm while also trying to be a good husband and father. Lost in his ambitions and disconnected from his deep feelings and real desires, Danny starts having nightmares and suffering from extreme anxiety. Doctors suggest medication. His wife gets worried and decides to leave the family home. Danny faces a big crisis. However, the fact that he sees his homeless uncle in his dreams every night and his intuition that his uncle plays some important role in this story urge Danny to embark on a journey to find his uncle and, more than that, to find his real self.

On his journey, Danny starts to get grounded, becomes more present and pays attention to the people and things around him. Slowly, he becomes more and more spiritual and starts to realise how things really work. He realises the importance of trusting his intuition and inner knowledge and observing the signs, coincidences or synchronicities leading him further down the path. From being superficial, he shifts and starts communicating in a more profound and honest way with other people in a way that he can touch their lives and they can touch his. Danny learns about energy healing, praying, divination and true spirituality. He also learns about homelessness and discovers the unlimited potential that we all hide within. When he meets his homeless uncle he learns even more about life and his mission and goes through an inner transformation that changes him in a very deep way. While reading Danny's story, we are reminded of the Journey of the Fool from the Tarot, who left behind all his material belongings and social life to embark on a spiritual journey and find his real self.

The story of the book is inviting every man and woman who feels lost in their work, mind and social roles to take a good look within, face their fears, connect to their desires, seek more knowledge and fulfilment and discover their mission in life. Everyone at some point has to do what is necessary to get to know themselves and transform their life into whatever they have always dreamt it to be. The challenge is big and the price can be high, but the result can be worth it. You can do it now, later, or even in another life, but you need to do it eventually. So, perhaps, the best moment to do it is now, in the present moment, because it is in the present moment that we only ever live.

# CHAPTER I

## The last Johnny with John – Getting it out of my head

John and I were friends since college. We studied and graduated from law school together. We even got married at the same day in the same church. We are now both successful lawyers earning healthy salaries and making our way to the top. We work for different legal companies in the same building. Sometimes, we even have some time in the evenings to share a quick cup of coffee before we meet clients or go to court to attend a case. The company I work for is called Success. Every Friday, I meet with John after work and have a few drinks. We talk about work and also share some news from our personal lives, you know... All this boring stuff that most married men at the age of forty chat about in a bar on a Friday night after work. But this Friday was different!

I was really messed up and, at the same time, determined to do something. I was having a nagging feeling that there is something I had to do urgently so I could get my life back together. I was also sensing that the more I delayed to do it the worse it would get. It was not that I wasn't happy with the money I earned at work. There was enough money to live a comfortable life and provide a comfortable life for myself and my wife Rosa, a caring and beautiful woman who I happily married some time ago. We used to have a nice happy life together until my nightmares started, followed

1

by negative feelings and emotional distress. There was something strange happening to me and I had lost my peace of mind. I couldn't sleep anymore, I had to seek therapy. Things were getting worse and worse and, on top of that, Rosa told me that she would leave the house. She said that she needed some time away from that madness, that it wasn't safe for her and the kids to sleep in the same place with me anymore.

The dreams I was having were always followed by a strange feeling. It was as if there was something more I had to do in my life. But the problem was that I didn't have a clue about what that could be. Things were getting worse and worse. Rosa, the love of my life, had left me and I was getting worse and worse. I had to sort it out one way or another; that made me talk to John that Friday. I needed to get it out of my head.

After I finished work, I headed to the bar close to our work in North Sydney, a highly industrialised modern suburb where our offices were. The bar "Elite" is the meeting place for many business people that work in North Sydney. John had supported me a lot both as a colleague and friend, and I was very anxious to talk to him. I went to the bar and thought of ordering a drink. However, I didn't feel like my usual whiskey. I used to have a few Johnnies every Friday with John.

After a while, John arrived. He greeted me and ordered two Johnnies. Then he gave me a tap on the shoulder and said cheers. It was then that I realised that my life had become a routine. It had become so predictable and mechanical as if I was following the script of a soap opera in which I had to repeat the same movements over and over again, while old couples were sitting in their couches half asleep watching it. However, I didn't want to be rude with him so I took the glass in my hands and started drinking.

"How did the case with the kidnapping go?" John asked me.

There was a case in which a mother had kidnapped her own kids and had asked for money from her rich husband, father of the kids, because she wanted to run away with her lover. I didn't feel like getting into details and just gave him a quick heads up about the case, as I was feeling anxious to talk to him about my issue. After finishing the whiskey and before John had a chance to order another round, I looked him in the eyes and said:

"John! There is something that I need to talk about mate; something that has been bothering me for a long time and I need to get it out of my head."

John seemed surprised hearing me saying that. He approached me and asked:

"How're things with Rosa and the kids?"

"It is still bad. Thank you for asking though," I replied.

"Do you have any problems at work?" John went on.

"Well if you let me speak, I can tell you everything," I said.

I know that was a bit rude to say that but I wanted to get his attention. I understood that it should be surprising and, perhaps, annoying for him to hear that I had something serious to talk to him about at the bar. But I did have something serious to share with him, so I went on.

"You see John, I know that you will probably think I am crazy or something, but I think I know what I have to do to fix things with Rosa and get my life back together."

And before John had any chance to say anything, I went on.

"I know that I am doing well at work, winning cases, earning money and all. I also know that I have been through a lot of stress lately. I broke up with Rosa and I am far away from my kids. While work is keeping me busy, I don't have to think about all my stuff all the time; but I still have this feeling... I hear a voice inside me telling me that there is something more I need to do in my life, somewhere I need to go so I can find myself. And while you may think that this is probably because of the situation with Rosa or because I am getting too tired at work, or disappointed with life I do not know... I have to tell you that this feeling seems like something much more important than that. It seems to be the answer for my problems."

The truth is that I hadn't planned exactly what I would say to John and I was trying, for the first time, to verbalize all those things that had been on my head for so long. And only by doing so, I was already feeling better. I was feeling as if I was changing the routine. I was breaking the invisible subconscious rules, shifting the conditioning and disobeying the self-imposed script of my life that had been making me more and more depressed. I felt that my life was taking a new course, that I was changing my destiny. I was taking back the power of my life, which would probably end up being a big failure if I continued living it in the same way. Even though I knew that John would probably get upset when he heard what I had to say to him, I still didn't care. I just wanted to talk to my best friend about my feelings, and I wanted him to listen.

I could see that John got really worried when I said all these things. He asked me if I wanted another Johnny. I didn't want. Then he told me:

"Look Danny, mate, we have been friends for years. We used to dream about life together. We used to chase girls together, remember?" We both laughed and John went on. "We fell in love at the same time and we got married on the same day, in the same church. I know you and you know me better than we know anyone else and that's why I will be honest with you, Danny. I will be honest because you are my mate and I love you, in a non-gay way always." I laughed out loud and remembered all the times he used to tell me that. John continued, "Danny, you seem very worried and stressed. I am afraid you are losing your mind mate. Look…" John paused for a while to take a deep breath. "… Look, Danny, you don't have to do anything crazy, my friend. You shouldn't put any more pressure on your shoulders mate. You are working fifty hours a week in a highly stressing, highly demanding and also, not to forget, highly-payed job. You broke up with Rosa a few weeks ago and you have been staying apart from her and your kids for quite some time now. If you have to do something, that should be taking some rest so you can feel better and maybe continue the therapy sessions you had started. So, please, stop telling this stuff to yourself about something important that you have to do and just relax mate. Take your time to get better. You know that we have worked very hard all those years in order to get where we are now; and that we truly deserve the money we are making and our comfortable lives. We both know very well that money does not grow on trees and that we had to work hard in order to earn all these things we own now. You also know Danny that we can pat each other's shoulder feeling damn happy and proud about where we are and what we have achieved so far. Now I know, mate, that things are not good for you and Rosa at this point, but let's keep thinking positive mate. Let's consider all of these just a crisis. Rosa loves you. I am sure you will get over whatever you are going through soon and you will get back together; and, by the way,

I reckon that we stop talking about all these now and drink some more Johnnies..."

When John said all those things to me, I felt that there was something wrong. I didn't use to be very observant when I was younger. I didn't use to pay attention to the body language, as I considered words sufficient to communicate and understand people and the world. I used to believe that our reasoning and our intellectual mind based on our past experiences and knowledge were enough to make evaluations and to know all we need to know about other people and life. However, as a lawyer I came across many clients and other people at work that kept lying and were trying to deceive me and deceive the judges. So, I gradually started paying more attention to non verbal communication and all these cues on an energy level that gave me hints about what a person really says and thinks. I started trusting more my gut feeling, relying more and more on this kind of communication and I got to know much more about people and their circumstances. I also started observing more the facial characteristics of people in order to look right through their eyes and into their hearts, so I could know the truth. I have to admit that I didn't do that only at work. I also started doing that in my personal life. And in that case with John, I felt that John was having similar doubts about the meaning of his life and that he was telling a story to himself so he could find the courage to wake up and go to work every day. He was projecting all his insecurities and fears to me, so he could find the courage to wear his nice suit and go to all these net-working meetings with all those important people that are all trying to make more money. It appeared to me that John had already gone through all these and that he had taken the decision to shut down this voice and ignore its calling, ignore his heart.

But my song was different than John's, and my voice unfortunately could not be shut down. And God knows how much I tried. I tried to shut it down every time by repeating words to myself. I really tried to convince myself that it was all good, until my nightmares began and my life fell apart very fast. Destabilising dreams started waking me up in the middle of the night in a state of total fear and distress. And, worse than that, I was feeling terrible in the following morning, when I started hearing this strange voice louder and louder within me, telling me that there is something more I need to do, and I knew that if I didn't do it, if I ignored that voice, I would end up being a caricature on my own puppet show. I knew I would find myself thirty years later, laying on my deathbed, looking back into my life and wondering if I could have done something different, wondering what would have happened If I had listened to that voice. And I was too scared to wait for so long to find out. I didn't want to waste away my life like that. I had already driven Rosa away and I was far away from the kids. I had no other choice but facing my fears and trusting my inner voice. I had to follow my heart and try to find myself again, so I took a deep breath, looked John in the eyes and said:

"Look John, I really appreciate your encouragement and kind words and yes, I do know that we deserve all we have, and that many people would envy a life like ours, a life that would appear so successful and privileged to many. And while I do understand that for someone like you that has matured so much, my feelings may seem premature or even idiotic, I still feel that THERE REALLY IS something more that I need to do," So, before John interrupted me (I saw in his eyes that he would) and started lecturing me again, I went on raising the tone of my voice and told him emphatically:

"The story is, John, that the last three years of my life I have been having this terrible nightmare. I keep seeing a homeless man, walking in a dark street, dressed in rags calling me every night in my dreams, and every time I wake up in the middle of the night feeling terrible for no apparent reason. Then, I try to sleep again and the next morning I wake up feeling so stressed, as if my whole life is wrong, as if it is a mistake and I have been hearing this voice within me telling me that there is something more that I need to do and that, as long as I am not doing it, I will keep having these nightmares, I will keep suffering. And, while I have been working hard all this time so I can get distracted and forget these nightmares, when I sleep at the night, I keep having them again and again. For the last three years, I have lived in a nightmare. I have tried so many therapies, even met a psychiatrist who suggested I take some sleeping pills and anti-depressants and you know, John, that I always used to run to the doctors every time I felt even the slightest pain. I always used to follow their advices and take all sorts of medications and pills. But this time, John, I have this deep feeling that I shouldn't follow the doctors' advice. I know that this feeling put my relationship with my wife and kids into risk, but I am willing to take the risk and find my way back to them."

John's face started to change while listening to my emotional speech.

"What are you thinking of doing?" He asked me.

"I don't know if I have told you about my uncle Tom, who left his home and went to live on the streets as a homeless many years ago. My folks hardly ever talk about him, but my father once told me that after Tom finished medical school, he started having some issues and, suddenly one day, he left his house and went to live on the streets of New York. My father tried desperately for many years to find him, but he didn't manage to. We know that he went to New York because of a Christmas card he had sent us three years ago and you know, John, it was when we got his letter that my dreams also began and I am more and more certain now that my uncle has something to do with my dreams. I feel that he might be the answer to my problems. You know, John, I think that finding my uncle and talking to him will help me solve the mystery, and get me back to Rosa and my kids."

John seemed to be getting very worried listening to what I was saying.

"I don't know what to say, Danny. I think you are driving yourself crazy by making up those stories in your mind and scratching old wounds. I'm very afraid that, if you decide to follow up with your crazy plans and go after a homeless man, you may lose any chances left with Rosa and your kids. Let aside the worry you will cause to your folks... So, you have to think it over very well, Danny, before you decide to leave everything behind and go after a crazy homeless man."

John went on speaking and even offered to pay for an expensive psychiatrist he knew so I could start therapy again. But John's reaction was not something that I did not expect. I didn't get upset or disappointed with him. I can't accuse people for not understanding me and trusting me and respecting my feelings and intuitions. I am the one who has to trust and follow them through. The way the situation was, I had to see the doctor again, take pills and suffer or trust my deeper feeling and go on with my plan to find my uncle in the streets of New York. Now that I have thought it over more, I know that I had actually taken my decision from before I talked to John. The next step would be the most difficult one: talking to my wife Rosa and trying to explain everything to her.

Rosa has been very supporting and doing her best to be patient with me while I was having those nightmares and all. But we reached a point which she could not take it anymore. She had to see me suffering every night while I was waking up terrified in the middle of the night. I was becoming more and more distant and it was very hard for her to deal with me. I was losing it. And, on top of all of that, I didn't want to follow the doctors' advices. Rosa couldn't understand; she was also very afraid for the kids.

Now, if I wanted to have a chance to stand as a whole honest and sincere man beside her, to truly honour and sweep her off her feet, as I used to do when we first met and fell in love, I would have to stay true to myself first and follow up with my feelings. That's why I had to talk to her and explain to her what I was planning to do.

That night at the Elite bar, I understood that I was not part of the elite and that I could not count on my best friend for his understanding and support, at least not in the way I expected him to do. I knew that if I wanted to detour from my life's movie script and take a different path, I would have to be by myself. I also felt that if I wanted to go out looking for my homeless uncle, I would have to go through tests, testing me in ways I couldn't even begin to imagine. The strange thing was that without knowing how, I had started to find the courage to move on. For some strange reason, this voice within me, telling me that there is something more I need to do, was also empowering me towards going on an inner and outer journey to find something that I did not know what it could be.

That Friday night, I said goodnight to John and patted him on the shoulder. I thanked him for taking the time to listen to me and for all the Friday nights we had spent together. I didn't hold any bad feelings for his reaction. He was just being himself as I had decided to be myself. Our paths were splitting. He would go back to work the next day and to the bar, possibly with some other colleagues, next Friday; and I would have to talk to Rosa and begin my journey.

# CHAPTER 2

# Talking to Rosa – Honesty comes with a price

That night before I slept, I was feeling really anxious. I knew that trying to talk to Rosa wouldn't be easy. On one hand, Rosa has a very kind heart; on the other hand, she is not the most patient and tolerant person in the world. I knew that talking to her about my plans to go away would probably upset and worry her even more.

The next morning, I woke up with a strange feeling. I felt scared and excited at the same time about my plans. I also felt anxious to talk to Rosa. While I was still in bed, I could feel my heart beating fast. I decided then to stay in bed a bit more. I stayed there lying with my eyes closed, and I started taking deep breaths to relax. Every time I had a stressful court case waiting for me at work, I used to do a breathing exercise that helped me a lot. I also did it every time I had to go through some stressful experiences in my personal life. I used to put my hands on my chest and try to breathe in fresh air and breathe out my fear and stress. Taking deep conscious breaths helped me to dissolve the fear and other negative feelings and restore inner peace and balance. My energy boosted up, I connected better to my body and heart and was able to think clearer too.

After I did my breathing exercise that morning, I got out of bed feeling already much better and more confident. I still knew that it wouldn't be easy to talk to Rosa, but I was more convinced about the necessity of doing it. I took a quick shower, drunk some fresh juice, ate some fruits and fresh yoghurt and got into my car. I drove to Bondi Beach where Rosa had moved back with her family at her parents' house. When I arrived there, I saw Rosa sitting on a rock by the beach. I approached her and gave her a big hug and a kiss in the forehead.

At that moment Rosa told me that she was thinking about when she met me. We were in our final year of law and I hadn't become an experienced lawyer yet. I was still a student, without a car, lots of money or a big name. My confidence and self-esteem were not particularly high. I did everything I could so she would notice me. I flirted with her in all possible ways. I flirted with her with all my heart and with total honesty. I bought her flowers and roses. Many roses. I wrote her romantic letters and took her for walks in nice parks and beaches where we would sit for hours talking about life and daydreaming together. When we got back home, we would call each other and talk for hours. I had been always honest with her. With time Rosa relaxed and started trusting me more, so she decided to leave back her past and make a commitment with me. I believe that my honesty and the way I talked to her radiating love were what kept us together also when we had to go through difficult moments, crises and conflicts in our married life. No matter what we were dealing with, we were always willing to put extra effort in order to find a solution together. Our love was really romantic, and we were still in love after many years of marriage, after having two kids. Rosa was still in love with me even when she decided to move away. And she knew that I was in love with her even though I didn't seem to want to do anything about our relationship. It was as if I was waiting for some miracle to happen so I could get better and be able to offer her and the kids a safe and healthy environment.

Rosa also told me how hard it had been for her to accept meeting me that morning. She was afraid that she would feel even worse seeing me after she moved out. But she wanted to see me though. She was also curious about my plans.

When Rosa saw me at the beach, I was already too close to her, hugging her and kissing her on the forehead. I sat with her then on a rock. She didn't feel like sitting there anymore, so she asked me to take a walk by the beach.

It was still early so the beach was quiet and the water looked wonderful. After a while, we found a nice spot by the rocks and sat there. I looked her in the eyes and said:

"Rosa, thank you for agreeing to see me in such a short notice. I hope I didn't make you worry, but there is something I have to tell you and I hope you will get happy hearing it."

Rosa was curious. She had established an emotional connection with me after all those years. It was as if there was an invisible cord extending from our hearts and connecting us to each other, picking up on each other's feelings and emotions.

"Have you decided to follow the doctor's advice?" Rosa asked me then.

"No, Rosa, I haven't. I don't want to start medication but, please, let me tell you what I have in mind. Rosa, my love, you know how much I love you, don't you? You are my heaven, my star… I am the happiest man in the world for having gotten married to you.

It was very hard listening to my heart-breaking words, but Rosa wanted to hear more so she looked me in the eyes, as a sign to go on.

"You know, my love, that I have been tormented over the last years by those strange dreams and that I have woken up in the middle of the night feeling scared and stressed. You know also how I wake up in the following morning always feeling horrible. Of course waking up beside you always made me feel better and helped me to pull myself together and move on with our day. I know how hard it was for you to be with me all this time. You had to go to work only with a few hours sleep as you were comforting me the whole night, when I was crying like a baby. I want to tell you now, my love, that I am convinced that I need to do something about that dream to clear it out."

"Of course you do, honey," said Rosa. "You need to do what the doctors have told you repeatedly. You need to let them help you."

"My love, drugs won't help me," I said.

"And what will then?"

"I have a hunch."

"A hunch?"

"Yes, a hunch?"

"What hunch? What are you talking about?"

"Do you remember my uncle Tom? He was the one who ran away many years ago and decided to live homeless in the streets leaving behind his work, family and the society in general. I have a feeling now that my uncle is somehow connected to my dreams and the strange feeling afterwards. I know it may sound crazy, my love, but I decided to go and find him in New York! I believe that this will help me to get better."

Rosa froze. Her eyes petrified and her face looked tensed. She stood up and said:

"You are kidding me right? Is it a joke? You have been suffering for all this time and I was there suffering too by your side. We have been to so many doctors and they all suggested to you to start medication. And instead of following their advice, so you can get better and we can keep our family together, you want to go to New York and look for your crazy uncle?"

Her question was less a question and more a hammer busting my head. I was feeling that it wouldn't get any easier. I had to listen, stay calm and explain.

"Look my love, I said, I know that it sounds crazy and I do not expect you to understand. I only expect you to trust me and give me a last chance. I want you to wait for me to come back."

Here it was. I had made my claim and the ball was on Rosa's court. I knew Rosa loved me a lot. What scared her more was the fact that I had taken a different path and decided to do something so different... That's why she was giving me a hard time.

"Look, Danny, I have been sleeping beside you all these nights when you were having those nightmares. I was waking up more scared than you every time you were waking up in the middle of the night, screaming and shouting. I have been trying desperately to calm you down when you were crying like a baby. I came with you in all your visits to all these doctors and I stayed there waiting for you. I was the one who kept telling you that you will be fine and we would get over that together. And, then, you decided to ignore the doctors' advice. That left me with no choice. I had to leave you, so I could protect our kids who were getting so worried with all these, but I was hoping that you would go back to the doctor and follow his advice. I was hoping that you would get better again and that we would leave all of this behind and be happy again. And now you come to see me to tell me all these nonsense about going to look for your homeless uncle. You scare me, Danny. I don't know what to say," Rosa started crying.

I did not know what to say either. I did not expect such a reaction. I expected an argument but not her crying. If I can't tolerate something in this world, that is Rosa crying. But I wouldn't give up. I had to stay loyal to my decision. I tried to hug her, but she pushed me away. I started stressing out again and immediately took some deep breaths and tried to calm down. The situation was worse than I expected and John's warnings about destroying my last chance to save my marriage were coming to be true. I approached Rosa and said in a low tone of voice:

"Rosa, I think that in life we have some priorities, don't we?" I didn't expect her to answer my question, so I continued talking. "…And for me my biggest priority is our family and love. And I know that you agree with that the most."

Rosa kept silent. She stopped crying and she had her back turned to me. I was sure that she was listening to every word I was saying, so I kept on…

"My love for our family, Rosa, is my biggest priority, and I would do anything for that, but there is something else that I need to have first in order to be able to ensure our family's well being."

Rosa turned to me and shouted:

"And what that would be?"

I paused for a few seconds and then said:

"Peace."

"Peace? What do you mean?"

"I mean that if we want our family to be fine and us to cope with life and all responsibilities and be happy, we need to have peace. And I don't mean only peace among nations, but peace of mind. Our society is full of unhappy, depressed people with anxiety disorders, stress and lots of suffering. People who have no peace. For some reason, so many people lack peace of mind, inner peace. I don't want to lecture you about the society's issues, Rosa, but I think we have to examine things very carefully here. When we were younger we had so many dreams, and so much strength and belief in ourselves to pursue them. We possessed a vivid imagination, and we tended to imagine our life the way we wanted it to be. We spent most of our days playing and doing what we loved and we didn't stress, worry nor fear about life. But, growing up and becoming adults with jobs, responsibilities, kids, bills and mortgages to pay added so many additional layers to that dreamer within us, to our inner child. We let our critical and imaginative faculties get worn out. Slowly, we became problems solvers and overstressed food addicts not even having time for each other as we used to.

"But that is natural, Danny. It is part of becoming an adult."

"No, its not. It's not natural to stop dreaming."

"That is called realism," said Rosa.

"The reality we construct is an illusion, Rosa, a nightmare created by our fears. By watching TV all day and following the news, we get nothing but bad news, disasters, robberies, murders, catastrophes, floods, bankrupts. Slowly the society converted us to fearful doubters of life, but life is magic. This puts out our fire Rosa and, if we dare to dream again or think a bit different than others, our friends and family are there to bring us back again to that fearful "reality" and crucify us in case we decide to follow a different path. When I met you Rosa, I was a dreamer, a romantic. I was full of energy to live life with you and fulfil all our dreams. Remember how we used to sit for hours together and dream... How we used to open our hearts to each other and share our deepest secrets... We weren't afraid of anything and anyone. We used to look in each other eyes and sense our souls' fire. And it was because of that fire that we fell in love. It was our souls that fell in love first Rosa, and then the rest of us. We didn't have time to think about it and decide rationally. We just followed our hearts and came close to each other. We started kissing and hugging and making love, making love with all our heart. But then, slowly, we became more and more afraid. We became too afraid to listen to our hearts. And, soon, we forgot our dreams. Now we are exactly like everyone else we know. We became puppets, having always to fulfil our friends and family's expectations; rushing through life to meet our work's deadlines. We have put our commitments before our dreams and desires. We became strangers to ourselves and then the nightmares started. Neurotic anxiety for no apparent reason. I call it dreams' killing. My unconscious mind, all my desires and dreams decided to rebel and flood my consciousness, a flood that is worse than all the floods we see in the news every day. I lost it Rosa. I don't know who I am any more. I don't blame you for leaving me. You did the right thing."

I said all this and looked deep into her eyes. I saw tears on her face. I continued speaking then:

"I know you still love me and you want me to get better but, Rosa, I have the feeling that I won't get better by taking pills. I need to follow my feeling and find my uncle. I know it sounds crazy and you probably won't understand, but I just wanted to be honest with you. I want to feel good again with myself, Rosa. I want to sleep again peaceful at night and find my inner peace. I know I had everything with you and nothing was missing and I want to get back with you more than anything. But in order to do that, I need to find myself again. I need to follow this calling and go find uncle Tom. I don't know why, but I feel that this will make the difference and I will be able to come back to you cured. If you could just wait for me, Rosa..."

Rosa looked me in the eyes. She seemed a bit relaxed; she always liked to hear me talking. I used to put her to sleep by reading her books. I used to talk to her through difficult emotional moments and this feeling of peace and love that emanated from our discussions seemed to emerge again, but she still seemed too scared and stressed out to trust my words and accept my decision to embark on this journey.

"So you think that by going away, you will solve the situation here?" Rosa asked then.

I thought for a moment, took a deep breath and then it came to me.

"Why don't you come with me?" I suggested...

"Are you crazy?" Rosa replied. "What about the kids?"

"My folks will take care of them. I will talk to them tomorrow. They always said they wanted to spend more time with them. So I am sure they would be happy."

Rosa seemed to like the idea.

"Ok. Let me think about it," she said.

I couldn't believe that I had asked Rosa to follow me to New York. One part of me felt disappointed that I might have to take Rosa with me, but another part felt happy because I could combine both going after my uncle and being with Rosa.

The next day, I would have to go and visit my father. My father hardly ever talked about my uncle. But I had to go there and ask him all sorts of questions so I could start my research. I knew it wouldn't be easy. I also knew that I had reached a point that I couldn't go back. If I stopped now, I would lose the faith in myself. I had to follow up with my last chance to get things together.

Rosa called me later that night and told me that she had decided that she wouldn't come with me after all. She started talking about me going to the doctor again. I told her one more time that I would go to New York; then, she said that she would stay with the kids and hung up.

I was feeling my energy depleted. I had to go along with my plan on my own. Maybe it was better that way, I thought. Rosa would be safer at home. I tried to raise some energy left and put myself together. I would have to visit my father the following day. I realised that I had initiated a movement that couldn't stop; I could only move forward. I felt like a wild horse, without breaks running into a dark highway without having lights or a clue about the destination. I just had this thought on my mind about finding my uncle and putting my life back together. This thought was becoming an obsession, a burning desire. I had to find the faith to support my emotions and follow my plan persistently. It seemed crazy, but it felt right within. That was the important thing, I thought that I should be trusting myself. Talking to my father would be the next step.

# CHAPTER 3

## Talking to my father –
## Scratching old wounds

The following morning, I woke up earlier than usual and had a quick shower. I have always treasured my morning showers before a busy day at work. Water always makes me feel better no matter how tired or stressed I am. When I am in the shower, I try to clear my mind from all thoughts and be in the moment. As the water runs through my whole body, I feel renewed as if it is removing all the negative energy and purifying my physical and emotional body. Water is the origin of all life. It seems to have a great healing capacity. So I had my shower and I really felt much better. I had a strong feeling that Rosa would relax over time and feel better and that my eminent meeting with my father would have a positive outcome as well. It had to! My father was my only hope to trace my uncle.

My father is a noble man, a man with traditional values, who always put his family above all. As an early migrant to Australia, he started from scratch and worked his way up to the top. He started as a book keeper and made his way up the corporate ladder of a bank, based only on his hard work, honesty and solid mathematic skills. He has always been proud of managing to advance financially so much in a few years, educating his children, taking good care of his family and staying loyal to his values. When I think of my father, I consider that we share the same loyalty, but for different things.

While my father has always put other people and responsibilities before himself, I have always tried to consider my feelings first and then those of other people. I knew that if I didn't do that, I wouldn't be able to maintain a good relationship with myself or with any other person. It was this loyalty that urged me to follow my gut feeling. I had this premonition to go after my homeless uncle, and I felt as if I didn't have any other option. I had to follow through. I couldn't turn my back to this feeling. What if my heart stops feeling anything else? What if I become totally numb living life only through my mind and physical sensations?

So, here I was knocking at my folks' door.

When the bell rung and my mother opened the door, she saw me and got very happy. I am her only son and I know she loves me dearly. Even though she liked her work very much, she decided to quit so she could raise me. By staying at home, she had an opportunity to raise me and also be a good housewife. She was cleaning, cooking, painting, making pottery and also collecting objects in her free time. I guess she has had a good life so far. But she has always wondered if she had made the right choice and how her life would be if she had continued working.

My mother started talking to me and after a while, I asked to see my father.

When I came to the living room, my father was still reading his morning newspaper.

"Hello, Dad."

"Hello, Daniel".

"What happened, dad? You seem surprised to see me here."

"Yes, I am, my son. At this time of the day... I am surprised indeed. Is everything ok at work?"

"Yeah, dad. Everything is fine at work. No complaints. As a matter of fact, I took a few days off."

"Oh, really?! That's good son, you need to take some rest indeed."

"Yes, I do. But I also want to ask you for a favour."

"A favour?"

"Yes! A favour..."

"Go ahead my son. You know you can always count on your parents. But tell me first... How is Rosa?"

"Rosa is fine, Dad."

"Good good! Nice to hear that, my son. And now, tell me… What can I do for you?"

"Ok. I have to tell you first then, that the reason I got a few days off work is because I am going on a trip overseas."

"A trip? How nice! And where are you going? If I may ask…"

"I am going to New York."

"New York? Why New York?"

"Before I tell you why I am going to New York, I would like you to promise to me that you won't get upset."

"Why would I get upset, my son? I know that you work very hard and I have been the one always telling you that you should take some time off and go for holidays, haven't I? But maybe you should also ask Rosa to join you. It will be a good opportunity for you two to spend some time together. You know Danny, I have been married to your mother for 35 years and I have never gone anywhere without her. I even paid for her tickets to join me on my business trips. We have travelled together all around Australia and I can tell you from experience that these are part of the proper values to keep a family together my son: respecting your wife, including her in your life, trying always to keep balance between work and family."

"I know Dad. I already asked Rosa to join me."

"Oh, did you?"

"Yes, I did."

"And what did she say?"

"She said that she is not coming."

"Why not?"

"Because… Look dad," I said with a serious look on my face… "I don't know how you are going to take it, but I have to be honest with you. The reason I'm going to New York is to find uncle Tom. I think he has something to do with my dreams."

"I can't believe my ears! You want to go to New York to find Tom?

Are you crazy, Danny? What is this all about? Why in hell have you thought about him? He has been the wound of this family for so many years. He has been the sins I'm paying for reasons that I am not even aware of. I have been honest and hard working for all my life. Our parents raised us both the best way they could. They gave us love and took care of us. They provided us with the best education and supported us in each step of our lives and, even though your uncle had a bright future ahead having just finished medical school, he has chosen to leave his house and everything behind, and live in the streets. You know, Danny, I don't want to talk about that. You know how much I cared about him and tried to find him and bring him back and you come to me now my son... You come... After all these years to tell me that you want to go and find him. Are you going crazy too, my son? I can't believe what I am hearing. Have you been drinking? What's wrong with you? Tell me... I... Did he call you? What happened? Please, tell me. I'm your father and I deserve to know..."

I could see that my father was out his mind and kept shouting at me.

My father was losing it. I knew it was entirely my fault. If I wanted to risk everything and go after my uncle, I should have done it alone without telling my father. I started questioning myself and my character. I was afraid I was making a terrible mistake. But then, again, I felt that maybe my dream and feeling to find my uncle may also help my father to find out more about him and perhaps come in terms with the past. I knew my father and how loving he was. I felt that he still had suppressed feelings for his brother hidden underneath his anger. I knew that he may never admit it, not even to himself, but he was still in pain and thinking about that gave me some courage and energy to go on.

"Look dad, you know that I have had all these issues over the last months with my dreams and I got struck by intense anxiety and destabilising stress. I have told you that I have seen the doctors and that they suggested that I should take sleeping pills since I couldn't sleep and my temper was getting worse and worse. I haven't told you, though that after I started feeling that my dreams had something to do with uncle Tom I started feeling better. My quality of sleep improved and the more I move forward and talk to people about it, think and plan about going and finding him, the better I feel. And now I am telling you that, if I want to find myself again, find peace of mind, if I want to restore my life, and stand as a real man beside my wife and kids, I need to follow up with this feeling. I can't live in such intellectual split any more, suppressing my unconscious and ignoring my feelings, Dad I need to stop all of this. I need to find uncle Tom and you need to help me."

My father looked at me very scared. He didn't know what to say. So I continued...

"Look, dad, you have two options. The first is too bury your head deep in the sand, keep resisting the reality of what has happened and keep suffering, and the second is to help me find uncle Tom so you get to know also about him and feel better. I know you Dad. You are a good man. You are kind-hearted and loving and, even though you have repeated to yourself and all others so many times you consider your brother dead, I know that deep inside you still have questions, you still want to know. You would like to help him still, if you could, wouldn't you?"

"And how are we supposed to help a man who decided to abandon his family, work, friends and society and live in the streets as a homeless man? How are we supposed to help him, if he doesn't even want to help himself?" My father was shouting at me... "How are we supposed to help someone, Danny, who doesn't want to help himself? And why should we do it? Why should we go through all this pain and suffering again when it was him who decided to leave us and live on the streets? Nobody made him choose that. It was his choice. We are not doctors or priests, Danny. We can't save him. You can't save the world. You only have to save yourself. You have to help yourself my son, to feel better and find yourself. You have to face reality and try not to escape it by making up stories in your mind. If you have issues, if you can't sleep during the night, we are all here to help you. We can find you the best doctors and pay for the best treatments. We can support you financially to stay off work as much as you need and get better. You may just need some time off. Why don't you take Rosa and the kids and go on holidays? We can help you with the tickets and all! What do you think?"

"I think that you don't want to understand dad, if I needed holidays I would just do that. Nobody has the same dreams for years because they are just tired of work. I may hate my work, but that's not the point now," I said.

I couldn't believe what I had just said. I had realised maybe for the first time that I hated my job. I guess it was my father's pressure that made me go deeper in myself and admit that I didn't really like my job. But, even though that piece of information could change many things in my life, I still knew that my dreams were much more than that. I knew that it was something bigger and it had to do with my uncle. So, I turned to my father and told him...

"Dad, if you love me and trust me, you have to help me. I know that we are not priests, but we are all creatures of God and we need to do our best to help ourselves and each other. We all deserve happiness. We all wish to avoid suffering. I know that you are afraid. You are afraid that I will run away like uncle Tom did, leave everything behind and end up in the streets too."

"And shouldn't I be? Your uncle was saying the same stories that you have just said, and it wasn't more than two days later that he disappeared. It was just like that. He didn't seem to be doing worse than you. He had just finished medical school and had a prominent career ahead, but he just left everything behind. He was probably having crazy dreams like you and mind issues."

My father was becoming harsh. He was very scared and in his attempt to protect me. He was giving me a very hard time, but I had to persevere.

"Look Dad, I understand that you are afraid. I am afraid too."

I went closer to him and said, then, in a lower tone.

"I have had issues, Dad, and I can't sleep during the night. I don't want to lose Rosa. I don't want to lose my children. I don't want to hurt you and Mum. I don't even want to go to New York and wonder in the streets, but I have a very strong feeling that I should do it. I should go and find him. It is not a decision that I took based on reason, something that I have given a great deal of thought. It is not something that I have analysed on my mind. It is a hunch, a feeling, an intuition, an attraction, a pull... I feel that if I want to find my peace and restore my life and find myself again, I need to do that despite all you fighting against me."

My father had to realise then that I wouldn't change my mind. I was too determined to quit. He wore his glasses and moved towards his big library in the living-room. He unlocked a drawer and pulled out a letter. With tears in his eyes, he gave it to me.

"This is from him. He sent it 3 years ago," my father said.

I looked at the date on the letter. It was about the same date that my dreams had begun.

"This was the last time we heard from him. Here, take it. It doesn't make any sense any way."

I took the letter in my hands and started reading it.

*Life is sometimes good here, sometimes it's bad.*
*Winter is cold and makes me freeze and flirt with death,*
*Other times it keeps me awake so I can see*
*the world the way it really is...*
*The summer is hot and makes me sick, makes me sweat.*
*Other times it keeps me warm and drives me to the beach.*
*The water makes me wet, when it comes*
*from the sky. It makes me cold,*
*and, other times, when I enter the sea, it*
*refreshes me. It makes me new.*

*I never feel lonely here. I am connected. I belong here...*
*I live in God's nest.*

*With love,*
*Timotheos.*

I got chills reading the letter. It sounded like a poem. It was my uncle's unique way to share his news, his life on the streets with his brother and family. It was his way to keep in touch. It was his poetic way to say to my father that he was ok. But that was something that my father would never accept. How can someone be ok in the streets, how can he belong there? I kept looking at the letter. I had the feeling that apart from the poetic words, the letter contained some information that would help me find my uncle. I examined it carefully with my full attention. Then, my work came to my mind. In many cases at work, we have to examine many types of evidence, written texts, letters, emails, messages and even pictures so we could recover information and gain insights about cases. Most of the written evidence we had to examine seemed to unfold in a similar way, they were following a particular pattern. They all started by providing general information and then while unfolding, they gave the important information or news at the end. Usually, in most of the written text, the most important information that would help us gain important insights about a case would be located at the end of the text. I have also noticed that most of the people do the same thing in their everyday discourse. In a simple sentence, story or paragraph we say or write, we often start with the general information and then at the second part of the sentence or end of the paragraph we provide the news, the most important part. So, I was holding the letter in my hands and was thinking of all this when I decided to have another read. It was then that I noticed the last sentence. It stood there spaced from the rest of the text, as if it was calling for my attention. It was in that sentence that the important information or news was. The information that could help me find my uncle.

*"I am connected. I belong here. I live in God's nest."*

My mind drifted away for a while. I tried to understand again what he meant by saying he is connected and he belonged. You would think that if you feel lonely, if you are not connected and you don't belong. What could a homeless man do? Someone who has a hard life in the streets and has to survive under the worst of the conditions? As soon as I realised that I was getting carried away again, I tried to focus on the sentence again. And then, my eyes rested on the last part:

*"I live in God's nest"*

Was it a religious message? Was it a teaching that my uncle wanted to pass to us? Or was it literal? We always try to read between the lines and decode language so we can discover the underlying meanings, but what I have also noticed at work is that many times the information we are looking for lies in front of our eyes. We just have to pay attention and look with a clear mind so we can recognise it.

*"I live in God's nest"*.

God's nest… Could it be an actual place? That's it! A surge of warm air penetrated my heart. I stood up, said goodbye to my father and headed to the door. Everything seemed to make sense. There is something more into all of this. My uncle was trying to pass some information to my father about his whereabouts. He had provided him with his exact location. His letter was a call that couldn't be answered because of my father's pain. He was too emotionally involved to read between the lines.

When I reached the door and I was ready to leave, my father shouted from the living room:

"Where are you going like that? What happened?"

"I'm going to God's nest!" I replied.

I knew that God's nest was the name of an actual place where my uncle had lived at least three years ago! I felt sure that I was holding the first piece of strong evidence about where to begin my investigation. My father seemed confused and worried. I thanked him again, opened the door and headed out.

I called Rosa on the way back home. She was at work. I told her that I loved her dearly and that I had managed to find a clue about where my uncle might be and that I would fly the following day to New York. Rosa told me to be careful. I felt good for a moment, I felt relaxed. I had a feeling that there was something out there helping me all the time. I called the airport and booked a flight to New York for the following day. I went back to my house and started packing. When I finished, I accessed the Internet and made a search for "God's nest New York". Five results came up. One of them had an actual address. It was a restaurant in a pub in a suburb near the airport. The following day, I would fly to New York and go the pub "God's Nest". Maybe my uncle was there.

# Chapter 4

## The flight to New York – A life changing experience

The following morning, I got a taxi to the airport. I took only a few clothes with me. I also didn't take lots of cash as I thought it could be dangerous to carry money on the streets of New York. While waiting to check in for my flight, I felt like calling Rosa again. I wasn't sure though if I should do that, since I didn't want to appear weak or say something that would annoy her even more. But I decided to call her anyway.

The phone rang and Rosa answered it. I told her once more that I loved her and that I couldn't wait to come back from New York. I told her that I was hoping that my trip would solve our problems and that we would get back together again… I really believed that.

I was hoping that Rosa could trust me after all that had happened… I was hoping she could find the way to trust me again. I seemed very confident on the phone. The way I spoke was different. Rosa told me that she loved me and wished me a safe trip. Talking to Rosa on the phone made me feel better. I knew that it would be hard to get things together and restore my relationship with her, but I had to move on. I tried to gather all my energy to my mission, which was to find my uncle while keeping myself out of trouble. I had to come back safe and sound for Rosa. I just had to find a way to do that.

During the flight I had a snack and then slept for a while. When I woke up, I remembered the book I had bought in the airport before I got into the plane. It was a book by a world famous psychiatrist named Carl Jung. His book was talking about coincidences. Coincidences that are part of our daily life and most of the people just dismiss them as luck. Jung's research about coincidences or synchronicities, as he called them, led him to believe that they are purposeful, that they have a deeper meaning. He described them as the union of internal (hunches) and external events in a way that it cannot be explained by cause and effect but it is meaningful for the observer. The author believed that there is a deeper reason, an underlying connection between these inner states and outer events that can be explained only if we assume the existence of a collective unconscious, a source of information in the open air or field where people can connect through their intuition or dreams and their unconscious and channel all sorts of information for people and even future events. I found the book fascinating and I was actually quite surprised to find out that there was scientific research about coincidences.

In my life so far, I had experienced a series of coincidences but it had never crossed my mind that they had any other meaning and I dismissed them as luck. While I was reading the book, I started entertaining the possibility that there is an underlying meaning for all our lives' events. What if a great power really exists? A collective unconscious as the author named it, which would help all to connect through our intuition, dreams and get guidance and healing? I started wondering if our lives are not guided by random events and luck but by a deeper force, a connection, a wise source that we could all use so we could find meaning in our lives. I started running on my mind the latest events of my life, my dreams and hunches about my uncle so I could start making connections. It was then that I started to see how my life had prepared me so far for this journey and had provided me with all the inner and outer resources and tools that I would need to complete this mission.

Before I even finished reading the book, a flight attendant came and asked me if I would like something to drink. I politely refused and sunk back into my thoughts, reflecting on all those "random" events and coincidences that I had experienced, trying to make more connections. Five minutes later, another flight attendant interrupted me again to ask me, if I would like to read a newspaper or a magazine. I told her to give me a magazine, hoping that I could get rid of her and sink back to my thoughts again. I was trying to figure out how all the coincidences of my life could be explained and reviewed under the perspective of synchronicities. I felt a bit dizzy, then, and I decided to have a look at the magazine. I opened it in a random page and it was then that I saw an advertisement at the bottom of the page: Pub &Restaurant "God's Nest:" I was totally amazed to see the name of the restaurant in a page of that magazine. "How could it be?" I thought.

I had randomly selected a book in the airport that I wouldn't normally get; a book about coincidences, and which provided a scientific view for these meaningful events. A few hours later, a flight attendant insisted on offering me a magazine that I opened in a random page that had an advertisement of the place in New York where I thought my uncle could be. A rush of energy penetrated all of my body, as I was convinced that there is a deeper meaning in all of this and that the more attention I payed, and the more alert I managed to stay, the more synchronicities would occur; the more I would be able to see the signs leading me further. In an instant, my whole life passed before my eyes, while I felt my heart getting warmer and my energy raising. A strong feeling of bliss, joy and ease entered my heart, as I was experiencing a sense of peace and clarity so strong that I had never experienced before. All the stress I felt, seemed to disappear. Suddenly, life started to appear magical to me. I thought that so far I was not a good student of life, but from now on I could do better. I would stop considering life events as random and resisting the flow of life. I would pay more attention, follow my heart, trust my intuitions and observe the signs or coincidences so I can receive guidance and healing from the universe. Suddenly, I had the feeling that my life was not worthless. It was not only for problem solving, surviving and accumulating money, but it had a deeper meaning that I could now focus my attention on. I started considering that my friends and the people I met in my life were not random and probably held important messages and information for me. I felt that Rosa was my soul mate and that we needed to help each other grow further together. I felt that I came to this earth, in this particular family, having these life experiences, for a deeper reason that had just started opening up to me. The idea of meaningful coincidences, a deeper meaning, a collective unconscious, a wise source, God perhaps, started changing the way I understood life. And, in a moment of clarity and joy, I could see myself changing from a highly stressed, worried and unconscious hopeless scared man to a fearless explorer of life, ready to embark on a journey of magical meaning and self discovery that would change my life forever. I felt that I was in the right place at the right time and that I was shifting gears and moving into a higher awareness and a more conscious perspective of life. I didn't know what exactly was happening to me, but I was experiencing a vivid transformation. I felt like a new person; my identity was changing and I felt I was awakening to the deeper truths of my existence. I kept my eyes closed and took some deep breaths trying to sustain that feeling of bliss, when the crew staff announced through the speakers that we were about to arrive in New York. I fastened my seatbelt, and prepared myself for the landing. I felt that the man who would arrive at the airport of New York was a different man from the one who got into that plane. Yet, it was still me. I could not understand very well what was happening, but I felt more confident and knew that I could trust the process. I knew that there is higher guidance and assistance from the universe and that I would need to start paying more attention so I could get guidance during my journey. I felt that I was awakening to my true potential.

When I arrived at the airport, I collected my luggage and took a taxi to the hotel.

When I mentioned the name of the hotel to the driver, he immediately told me about the amazing soup they make in the Pub near there. I was surprised that the driver mentioned the Pub and thanked him for the information. I had a smile on my face and felt my eyes shining as if I had just won the lottery. I asked the driver, then, about how safe the area near the hotel was.

"Look, the place is nice, he said. And the hotel is good. You just have to be careful not to carry lots of cash with you in the streets."

"Oh really? I hope nothing bad happens to me."I told him then.

"Yeah! There are many homeless around the hotel and pub. I guess you wouldn't like to be robbed, would you?"

"Are you aware of any incidents with homeless people, similar to the ones you describe?" I asked him.

"No, I don't. Look, I try to do my job here and not to poke my nose into their business. It's safer that way. Trust me. I would advise you to do the same…The people in the streets know me by now. They know that I'm just doing my job and I have never had any problems with them. But you are a foreigner, so you'd better be careful…"

"But do you know anyone that has had any problems?"

"To tell you the truth, no, I don't, but it's common sense that it is dangerous to wander with cash in a street full of homeless people, junkies and thieves, isn't it?" The driver said.

I nodded my head and started getting lost on my thoughts again. I started thinking, then, that it wasn't very nice what the taxi driver had just said. He was speaking about the homeless in the same way he spoke about drug addicts and criminals. He has probably been in the streets as a taxi driver for so long and the homeless haven't done anything bad to him. Why was he grouping them together with thieves and junkies, then? It seemed unfair…

"But why do you want to know about the homeless people here?" The driver asked me, then.

"My homeless uncle has been living near that area, and I am going there to look for him."

"Oh, really!? I feel bad, now, for what I had said before. What if all homeless people are not the same…What if some of them are different? What if some of them are there by choice? But again, what is choice? We live in a society and end up having manufactured choices that are not really our choices. They are choices that come out of conditioning, self limiting beliefs and brainwashing. We are all shaped by our families, friends, and past experiences, by the media, the government, and the culture we live. Has your uncle chosen to live in the streets?"

"Yes, I guess he had." I replied and decided to tell him a story from my work.

In Sydney, I work as a lawyer. Once, I had a client who decided to leave his family and start living in the streets after losing his job and not being able to get a new one. He felt ashamed, and didn't want to be a burden to his family, so he decided to leave them and start living on the streets. His family and wife did everything possible to find him and bring him back.

When they finally found him, they convinced him to come back. They came to me, then, and asked me to help them claim funds from his last job because he had been fired inappropriately, without a serious reason or even compensation. The man was so desperate and afraid after they had laid him off; afraid of having to support a wife and two kids and believed he was not worthy of anything and "chose" to run away to the streets. It was not that he didn't really have any other choice. He could have stayed home close to his wife and kids and try to find a solution. He could have asked his wife to find a job and contribute financially until he could find a job again. But because of pride, fear, negative beliefs and stereotypes, he chose to live as a homeless person.

The driver listened to my story carefully and started thinking why that man in his taxi was telling him all of this. Even though it was an extreme case, it made him think more about the choices we make every day that are not really our choices. He chose to drive this taxi not because he really wanted, but because his father gave it to him and convinced him that it was a good job. "It will ensure you financially", his father said. "You will never get hungry, my son."

"You know, my choice to become a taxi driver was not really mine, but my father's suggestion. I always had an interest in philosophy and wanted to know more about human soul, but because of fear I "had chosen" the easiest solution, which came from my father's influence. Maybe your uncle's choice to live on the streets was a similar case. You know what? I will go to the library after my shift and borrow some philosophy books, so I can start reading again. I can even discuss my ideas with my clients in the taxi. I can even go back to university and study philosophy, who knows? Maybe I can make new choices now. Yes I can. I know I can!"

Soon the taxi arrived at the hotel. I thanked the driver, paid him for the ride and gave him an extra tip for his assistance and his politeness to talk to me and answer my questions. He seemed very happy. When I entered the taxi an hour ago, the same man seemed moody and tired and had an empty expression on his face. An hour later, he looked like a different man. His face was shining and he was wearing a big smile. That made me think how some small gestures can make the difference for the people we meet in our lives. I thought that if we took the focus from our little selves and started paying a bit more attention to everyone around us, noticed their feelings and tried to make them feel better, it could make the world of difference in their lives and in ours too. I started seeing things from a different perspective. I felt I had initiated a process of growth and awareness that could transform my life forever. I tried to keep my focus on my mission, though, which was to find my uncle and bring him back home. At the same time, I couldn't wait to go back home and hug Rosa. I wanted to tell her and everyone else about all of my experiences and all the changes I had experienced. I thought that if everyone started paying more attention to the coincidences and recognised the guidance of the universe, it could make all the difference in their lives. We could all become aligned!

# Chapter 5

## God's Nest – A bowl of hot soup

By the time I arrived at the hotel, I was feeling very tired. I quickly checked in, went straight to my room and laid in bed. I fell asleep very quickly and had the same dream again. I dreamt about the same homeless man. This time I was close to him and I was approaching him more and more. I tried to make out his characteristics, when I suddenly felt the ground moving away from my feet and I found myself back home with Rosa. When I woke up I felt confused. I knew that I had to find my uncle so I could end this story once and for all and stop having these nightmares. I got out of the bed and put on some old clothes so I wouldn't attract too much attention walking in the streets. I had decided to walk to the pub. I went down to the reception and walked straight to the door. The doorman asked me how I was.

"I am fine, thanks. How about you?"

"I am good sir, thanks for asking. Would you like me to call you a taxi?"

"Well, it depends. How far is it to God's Nest?"

"God's Nest?"

"Yeah! The Pub near here…"

"Oh! Ok, yes. I understood. Sorry. It is close, but I'd better call you a taxi."

I knew it would be safer to take a taxi, but I still wanted to walk. So I thanked him and told him that I would walk there.

I knew that he was trying to do his job and I walked out of the hotel and started walking alongside the pavement when a few yards away from the hotel old buildings started to appear. The street lights were slowly fading away as I was making my way to the pub, making the street appearing dark and threatening. I tried to keep my attention to the street and relax. I could see piles of litter with some men that could barely be seen lying on top of it. Some of them were using garbage bags as pillows. For some strange reason, I wasn't afraid. I was feeling safe. I don't know why, but I had a strange feeling that they couldn't see me, as if I was invisible. I felt that if I managed to keep my energy balanced and if I didn't endure to negative emotions of fear and desperation, I would be safe, I wouldn't be noticed. I heard some people talking to each other in a small alley. They seemed young and their faces looked really ugly and mean. I thought they may have been drug smugglers or thieves, wandering on the streets looking for innocent victims. I stopped looking at them and kept walking straight while taking deep breaths. After walking for a few yards more, I could finally discern the pub at the end of the street. I went straight in. When I entered the pub, I took a deep breath and felt grateful for not having been attacked out there.

The pub seemed to be decent for the area it was in and the people inside seemed ok as well. I thought that people should drive or take a taxi to go to the pub. I was the only one crazy enough to go there on foot. I had a look around then, and headed to the bar. When I approached it, the barman smiled at me and asked me if I wanted something to drink. I nodded and told him that I was hungry, so he passed the menu to me. I didn't even look at the menu and asked for some soup. He seemed really surprised that I ordered the soup and asked me:

"How do you know about that? Had you ever been here before?"

"No, I hadn't," I replied. "I've just arrived in New York."

"Sorry, I don't want to be nosy." he told me then and continued:

"But the reason I am asking you that, sir, is because only regular customers know about our soup. Our chef makes an amazing hot soup with all sort of vegies and mushrooms and only regular customers know about it and order it as the soup is not even in the menu. So when I saw you ordering the soup, I thought that it couldn't be a coincidence and that you must had been here before."

I told him that the taxi driver that brought me from the airport to the hotel had told me about the soup.

"Oh... how come the taxi driver mentioned the pub?"

I looked at him trying to decide if I should trust him or not, then I said:

"Look, mate, the reason I'm here is because I'm looking for my uncle. He left home many years ago and we got some information recently that indicates he lives around here, close to the pub.

"So your uncle is a homeless?" he asked.

"Yes, he is… I guess you could say that as he lives in the streets."

"And what's your uncle's name?"

"His name's Tom".

"Tom…" He said trying to think if he had heard of his name before. He continued:

"Hmm... I know a few homeless that live around here, but I don't know anyone with the name Tom."

"And how do you know those homeless?"

"They come here once in a while when they have money to buy some hot food and drinks. Some of them help us to take the garbage out and move things in the basement. We know them well by now and we trust them, so we let them help and give them food, clothes and some money in return."

"Maybe your uncle has changed his name," the barman said. There are many homeless around here that don't use their real names on the streets. They use nick names. Your uncle may be one of them…

I took a photo out of my coat and showed it to him.

"This is a photo of my uncle. He sent it to my father for Christmas three years ago. He also sent us a letter which mentions the name of the bar."

He seemed amazed to hear that.

"What does the letter say?" He asked me.

"It says that he lives in God's nest!"

The soup arrived at that moment, but I was too anxious. So I kept asking him if he recognised the person in the photography.

"No, I don't," he said. "I am really sorry, but let me ask if someone knows him." He headed to the small room which seemed to be his boss' office.

When the barman went into the room to ask his boss about my uncle, I was feeling very anxious to see if he would recognise him. I was hoping that he would come out of the room with some good news for me. I decided to try the soup, then, while waiting for him to come back.

The first sip of the soup made me relax a little. It was very tasty, hot and creamy, exactly the way I like it. It had mushrooms and a variety of vegetables, small cut pasta and various spices in it. Every sip of the soup tasted better and better, as it was leaving a combination of a sweet and sour taste in my mouth. My body got warm and I was getting more and more relaxed. I knew from before that food is the primary source of energy and the key aspect of health, but when I was working I always used to eat in a hurry. I never had enough time to take my time and enjoy a meal. I used to eat fast-food without paying any attention while eating. I just used to swallow my food while discussing about law cases with colleagues, or working on some case on my laptop. Even at home with Rosa, we didn't use to cook a lot. We preferred to go to fancy restaurants and spend a fortune to eat fancy dishes. But, that simple soup brought me back to my childhood, when my mother used to prepare a similar soup for me. I felt rejuvenated, relaxed and my energy was rising. All the fear and stress I was feeling seemed to be fading away. I couldn't believe how a bowl of hot soup could do all this magic to me. It seemed to have come at the right time to distract me from my fearful thoughts and bring me back to the present moment. I could feel nice and peaceful again.

When the barman came out of the room, I had already finished my soup. I was much more relaxed and noticed that the barman seemed to have felt sad for not being able to help me with my uncle. Neither his boss nor anyone else in the bar recognised my uncle in the photo.

The barman approached me then, and told me that maybe my uncle had changed after those years in the streets and it was for that reason nobody could recognise him.

"It happens here a lot with the homeless..." he said.

"Is there any basement in the building?" I asked him.

"No, there isn't." He replied.

I started getting anxious again.

"Do you think I could talk to those homeless men when they come here to help you?" I asked him.

He thought for a moment and then told me that it should be ok. He also told me that he knew these people for quite a lot of time and they were nice and they wouldn't mind helping me.

"There are some homeless coming here tomorrow to help us move some furniture." the barman said.

"That's great! I can't wait to meet them. Thank you so much."

"You don't have to thank me. I am happy to help," he told me.

I was very surprised to see the bartender so willing to help. Until now I thought that bartenders are supposed to serve drinks only, not to help solve people's problems. I guess I was wrong. This bartender seemed to be a very nice person, and he seemed to be rather used to help other people. I started thinking then that, in my job as a lawyer, I had worked for many years with many highly educated and successful people, but I had never came across people that were willing to help, people who would care enough to help someone in need. Money and success were their primary motivations. And here I could meet this barman who works in a simple pub in New York, serves amazing veggie soups and helps people. "How amazing!", I thought and how lucky I was to be in that particular place at that particular time and talk to him.

It seems that since I have started paying attention to everything and everyone around me, I have been constantly meeting nice people. Or was I attracting the good side of all the people I met? What if my new state of mind and consciousness helped me attract the good side of all people I came across so I could get guidance and help? Maybe if I had thought like that before and given energy to the higher selves of everyone, my life would have been much better. Maybe I wouldn't have ended up going through all these issues and driving Rosa away.

It was getting late and I decided to leave. I thanked the bartender and told him that it was a pleasure to meet him. I paid for my soup and gave him a small tip. He thanked me back, smiled at me and said he would see me in the following day at 7am. It would be an early wake-up for me, so I decided to go back to the hotel and get some sleep. He called me a taxi and I got back to the hotel very fast. I laid on my bed and started taking deep breaths, trying to balance my energy and relax. Soon, I had fallen asleep.

During my sleep, I dreamt about the homeless man again. This time I could see him even better. He looked like an angel. He approached me and looked me straight into the eyes. I couldn't see his face clearly, but his eyes were big and intimidating. I woke up. It was 5 o' clock and I couldn't sleep any more. I felt agitated. It was as if I was approaching my uncle and he knew it. I felt I was getting close.

I got out of bed and took a hot shower. The water relieved my stress and raised my energy. While in the shower, I closed my eyes and tried to visualise the rest of the day. I got an image of the group of homeless people in the pub helping with the furniture and I was talking to one of them. I opened my eyes and got dressed. I couldn't wait to go to the pub again and talk to them.

# CHAPTER 6

## Praying for the first time

It was 6:30am when I left my room. I took the lift down to the reception area and asked them to call me a taxi. I arrived at God's Nest at 6:55am and saw Michael, the bartender, at the door talking to some people. I walked towards them and said good morning.

"Good morning Danny." The bartender replied.

"How are you today?" I asked the homeless man.

The homeless man replied:

"I'm good thanks. Michael was explaining to us how to move some boxes with care so we don't break anything. He told us that you are an old friend of his and that you have been looking for your uncle who has been missing for many years."

I nodded confirming Michael's story and tried to appear cool. I didn't want to scare them away because of my anxiety to find my uncle.

"I'm here looking for my uncle. We used to be very close some years ago, but then he had some issues and disappeared. I think that he is around here on the streets, so I decided to come by and ask around."

"And why do you want to find him? If he left, it means that he may need some time away from everything. He needs some privacy."

"I know, I know I replied. I just need to see him. I think he may need help."

He seemed to have gotten upset hearing that.

"And how do you think you can help him?" He asked me and continued speaking without giving me time to reply:

"If he decided to come to the streets, it means that he may not want your help. Don't you think?"

"I just want to tell him that we love him and that he has my support in case he needs something. That's all." I said.

"If you really love your uncle, you'd better give him some space." He insisted.

I realized that he wouldn't help me. He didn't seem to believe I was truthfully saying what I wanted. I thought for a moment and said:

"Look I am listening to what you say and I really understand you, trust me. I don't want to cause any trouble or disturb my uncle or anyone else. My uncle has always been a difficult person and I have always respected him and gave him space since I was a small child. I knew that this was the only way to stay close to my uncle. The thing is...". I started saying that my uncle and I had a business together and when he decided to leave I lost some important contacts. Now I was really in trouble and I needed his help to get back on my feet. I said to the man looking into his eyes:

"I need your help."

He, then, asked me what my uncle looked like.

I took the photo from my pocket and showed it to him.

He looked at the picture and then said to me:

"I think you are lying about the whole thing."

I looked at him, deep into his eyes and said:

"You know you should trust me."

"Look, I would really like to help you, but I don't know the man in the picture."

I came close to him, raised the tone of my voice and said:

"Look, I have come a very long way from Australia to New York to find my uncle. I am holding a letter in my hand that he sent us three years ago saying that he is here, in God's nest. So, please, you have to tell me the truth. If you know my uncle, please help me find him." Then, I showed him the picture again.

"And how do I know that you are not going to cause any trouble for him?" He asked.

"You just know it," I said. You can see it into my eyes, can't you? I have good intentions.

He looked at me and said:

"I know that you are not telling me all the truth, but I can also sense that you have good intentions indeed."

He took the picture of my uncle and gave it another look.

"Well, now that I am looking at the picture again, it reminds me of a friend here with the name Tom." He told me then. "By the way, my name is Peter."

"So you know my uncle?" I asked him raising the tone of his voice even more. "Do you know where he is?"

"Well, I don't know where he could be. All I can say is that Tom likes to travel a lot. No one can understand how he manages to travel so much. You know, your uncle is a legend here in the streets. All the homeless community know him. He has helped the community a lot."

"You mean that my uncle is famous here?" I asked. "Why? What does he do?"

"Look man, you will forgive me but I can't say anything else. You have to find out by yourself. You have to be ready. You may find yourself in a big surprise. Tom has a lot to say."

I was confused. I said:

"Look, I need some more help. I need to find out where he is."

Peter told me, then, that I wouldn't have to do that.

"Your uncle will find you first when the time is right. Since you are here and have the intention to meet him, he should know it by now and he will probably appear in front of you very soon. Just be patient and wait."

I got even more agitated.

"What are you talking about?" – I asked. "I don't want to be rude, but what you are saying is crazy. Are you kidding me? ... As if my uncle has special magical abilities to know where I am and what I want. My uncle is a homeless, you know. He is not a medium," I said.

Peter laughed loudly.

"Your uncle lives in the streets, but he is not homeless and, yes, he has abilities," he replied. He has helped the community a lot. He even helps outsiders, you know... guys like you that have a good job, a house and everything you need. He has helped guys that have everything apart from peace of mind."

"And my uncle offers peace to people?" I asked. "How does he do that?"

"Well, as I said, you will have to find out for yourself," Peter replied. "Patience is the biggest virtue. You have to be patient." He said and left heading back into the pub.

I followed him into the pub where we found Michael and the others. They were trying to lift a fridge. I helped them move it and then I said to Michael what Peter had just told me. I asked Michael, then, to tell Peter to give me some more information about my uncle.

"Look, Danny," Michael said. "if my man Peter here said that your uncle is out and around and he will find you, then maybe you should try to relax and do that."

I couldn't believe what was happening. I felt that they were making fun of me. I had come all this way, left my wife, kids and family behind to come to New York so I could find my uncle. And now that I was getting so close, they were trying to convince me that it was better to sit back, relax and do nothing, just wait for my guru uncle to track me down with the power of his mind. How could I accept that? Sure, I had discovered that there are more things in life than I had learnt or imagined before. Yes, there are signs offering guidance in our lives. I have realised how important it is to stay alert and pay attention to everything around so we can notice the synchronicities and receive guidance and healing. I had also understood how important it is to give value to everyone we meet so we can attract their good side and get important messages. But now having to accept that my homeless uncle had powerful abilities and was an important man who would guess where I was and find me first... That was too much to accept.

I left the pub feeling upset, got into a taxi and went back to the hotel. I was very anxious and scared because I started thinking that I had come all this way for nothing. I was losing my faith.

I started thinking then, what if I was deluding myself all this time to believe in magical coincidences and ghost stories? I didn't know what to do. My energy was dropping and I was feeling small and powerless. Then the image of Rosa came to my mind. I thought I should call her and tell her about my trip. I used the phone in the hotel room and dialled her number. She answered the phone a few seconds later. She seemed happy to hear my voice and asked me if I was ok. I told her that I was fine, and that I was staying in a nice hotel near the pub. I told her that I had met some people that had seen my uncle around. I also told her that I had learned from one of them that my uncle was known on the streets and that he had helped a lot of people there. Rosa asked me when I would come back home. I told her that I would go back soon and that I had to stay there a little longer to find my uncle. I told her that I was getting very close to that. I didn't know if I was lying or not. There was a voice within me telling me that I was getting close indeed to find my uncle, and another telling me that, perhaps, I was kidding myself. I decided to listen to the one that made me feel better.

After I spoke to Rosa on the phone, I was already feeling better. I felt like an investigator trying to solve a mystery. My energy rose again and I tried to take some deep breaths so I could relax even more. Then, I felt my stomach complaining and I decided to go down to the restaurant and order something to eat. While I was sitting in the restaurant I had a strange feeling that the homeless guy could be right, that I should stay alert and pay attention to the signs that would lead me further. After finishing my dinner and drinking a glass of wine, I headed back to my room, laid on the bed and closed my eyes. I started taking deep breaths and trying to empty my mind and relax, then suddenly I started seeing myself going out in the streets again looking for my uncle. I felt a strong pain in my stomach as if someone had struck me with a stick. I got very scared, but I kept breathing deeply, sending energy to my heart and trying to push away the fearful thoughts and negative emotions. I knew that it would be dangerous to go out in the streets again looking for my uncle, but I decided to take the risk. I wouldn't stay there in my room doing nothing. If I had made all these sacrifices and had gone to all this trouble to come all this way, I wouldn't stop now. I was still very afraid despite my willingness to go out in the streets and look for my uncle, but I was determined to take the risk.

Then, without thinking, I felt like praying. I was never a religious person and I had never prayed before. I realised though that there is something bigger out there guiding us. There is a higher intelligence to which you can connect so you channel information and healing. I felt that I had to acknowledge this power and ask for help. For a moment, negative thoughts came to my mind. I though that I was being desperate and weak, but my urge to pray was so strong that I decided to go ahead. As I had never prayed before, I didn't know what to say. I started by apologising for that. The rest of my praying can be resumed in the following lines:

*I would like to express my deepest gratitude to the Universe and Higher Intelligence for all the assistance and guidance that I have received so far. I ask for guidance and protection in my endeavours to find my uncle and for the highest good of everyone involved.*

After I said these words, I remained in silence for a few moments, breathing deeply and trying to shift my attention within myself. When I opened my eyes, I was feeling very peaceful. My heart was warm and I felt that same nice feeling that I had felt in the plane during my transformational moment when I discovered the synchronicities. I could feel that I was guided by a higher force all the way. I felt ready to go out and look for my uncle. I thought that if Peter the homeless guy was right and my uncle would locate me first, maybe I should still be on the go and follow the signs. I had to show my intention to the Universe. I had to show that I really wanted to see my uncle and even take risks for that. I got off bed, put on some old clothes and made my way out of the hotel.

# CHAPTER 7

## Hard times and natural healing

So here I was out in the streets again making my way to God's Nest. I couldn't stop thinking that if my uncle had said that he was in God's nest, then, he might as well be there. I passed through the same alleys that I had crossed the other night, but I felt much safer now, maybe because it was still day time. It is funny how the same place can appear so different, depending on both internal and external conditions. In that case both the fact that I was feeling more relaxed and brave and also because it was still day, made the place seem much safer and more alive than it seemed two nights before.

Soon, I arrived at God's Nest. The pub was closed and no one seemed to be there. This could be a good chance for me to do some searching around, I thought. So, I started looking behind the pub and around the establishments of the old building that during the day seemed more like an old house than a pub. I was trying to discern if there were any hidden passages or other places in which people could hide and use as a shelter. It was then that I noticed a small alley next to the building. The alley was covered with leaves and garbage and it seemed to lead behind the pub. I used my hands to remove some of the garbage so I could move through the small alley. While I was crossing the tiny alley, I could hardly fit through the walls. I started hoping that I was about to discover a hidden shelter. When

I reached the end of the alley, I saw an old mattress thrown on the ground and some broken glass. It didn't seem like anyone was staying there, at least not for some time. I couldn't believe that I had reached another dead end and I started looking for some other hole, hidden passage or way that could lead under the building, under God's Nest.

Suddenly I heard noises. Two men were talking loudly and their voices indicated a relatively young age. I thought that I should stay still where I was in case the men were criminals, drug smugglers or thieves. I was afraid that if they discovered that I was there, they would harm me. In my efforts to move back a little so I could hide better, I stepped on some broken glasses and made some noise. The men heard the noise and stopped talking. I was scared to death as I was hearing their footsteps approaching me. They were walking towards me. I tried to stay calm, but I was sensing that I was in great danger. I didn't have anywhere to go or hide. The way the guys looked confirmed my fears. They were wearing black sunglasses, black jackets and they had hoods covering most of their faces. They probably had been smuggling drugs, guns or doing some other dirty business.

"What are you doing here man?" Asked one of the thieves.

"Oh, I was just cleaning the pub and heard glasses breaking outside, so I came out to have a look."

"That's bullshit man, cut the crap. Are you looking for trouble? Look man, this is our hood and no one hangs out here without paying a commission to us, if you know what I mean."

"Look mate, I only have a few dollars with me, so just take it and leave me alone, please."

"Shut up," said the other thief pulling a knife out of his jacket and pointing it to me. And he continued:

"You want me to open you up?" He asked raising the tone of his voice, trying to show me that they weren't afraid. It was only the three of us there.

"Now tell us what the hell you are doing here." He asked me raising his voice, almost shouting.

"Ok, I will. I am looking for my uncle and as I had information that he was somewhere around here, I came to look for him."

"You have to be kidding us man." He told me, then. It seemed that he didn't believe me and the fact that I had supposedly lied made him crazy. I started getting even more scared and started moving towards them so I could run away. I said:

"Look, I am just getting out of here, ok?" and continued walking towards them.

Then, all of a sudden, I felt a strong hit on my head. One of the thieves had hit me with a piece of wood. I was dizzy, but still felt another strong hit and, then, I lost my senses. Later I found out that I had been hit all over my body and had had my wallet stolen.

The first time I opened my eyes after the incident in the alley, I realized I was in a small room of what seemed to be like a temple or something. I immediately thought, then, that the guys had probably kidnapped me and took me there so they could continue to torture me and probably get more money from me. I thought that I should try to get out of that place and go straight to the police. When I tried to move, I felt pain all over my body. All my muscles and bones were aching. I realised then that I was badly hurt. I had a terrible headache and many parts of my body seemed to be wrapped. I felt like crying, but I took a deep breath and tried to reach a half empty glass of water that I could see on top of a small coffee table next to the bed I was laying in. I managed to reach the water and, as I was very thirsty, I drunk it fast and tried to get out of the bed again. It was then that I heard the door opening and a young man coming in. He had Asian characteristics. He approached the bed with a smile on his face.

"Hello, my friend, are you ok? How do you feel? You'd better not to move."

"I am not ok." I replied. "I don't know where I am and who you guys are, but you should know that I am a lawyer and many people know that I'm here. So, they should be looking for me and the police will soon find out where I am and come here."

"Relax Danny," the guy said.

I felt astonished hearing my name. I thought they should have found my credit card or ID. Then, I remembered that I didn't have my ID with me, I had left it in the hotel.

"Where am I?" I asked the guy. "What is this place?"

"We found you in the corner of an alley close to a pub. You were bleeding and laying there unconscious. You seemed to have been bashed and thrown there. We searched for your ID but your pockets were empty. We, then, decided to take you from there as quickly as possible and brought you here."

"And why didn't you call the police or get me to a hospital?" I asked in a threatening tone.

I was still shocked and I had trouble to believe his story. For some strange reason though, the more I talked to him and started paying attention, the more I realised that he didn't look like a criminal. He was dressed in a traditional attire and looked like a monk.

"Are you part of some religious cult?" I asked him. "Have you been capturing innocent people?"

"Actually..." the Monk replied. "...we are normal people like you Danny, working in the area and since we found you and you were in the need of help, we tried to do the best for you."

"So, why didn't you get me to the hospital?" I asked him again.

"Look..." the monk replied retaining a relaxed tone of voice "...we would have taken you to the hospital but there was no taxi around and we thought that by the time we found transportation to get you there it might have been too late. You seemed severely injured and you had already lost a lot of blood and you seemed to have broken a few limbs as well."

"So, how did you treat me then?" I asked. "Are you a doctor?"

"No, I'm not a doctor." The monk replied. "But..."

"But what?" I interrupted. "Look, don't play with me. Can't you see that I'm in pain? I should go to the hospital straight away."

"If you want to go to the hospital, we can arrange to get you there as soon as possible." The monk said. "Actually, I can call a taxi for you right now. The thing is that your injuries do not appear to be only physical. That's why we thought it would be better for you to stay and heal here."

"What do you mean by that?" I asked.

"We think that you have gone through a lot lately and that you may experience post traumatic shock and emotional trauma along with your physical injuries. That's why we thought that if you stay here we can work with you in a holistic way."

"What do you mean by that?" I had to repeat the question. "Holistic way? How can you treat me emotionally and how did you attend my physical injuries if you are not a doctor?"

"You seem really stressed out Danny and we knew that you would be like that when you woke up." Said the Monk. "I think you should try to relax because of your condition. You are recovering and in order to help you with that, please, let me explain everything to you."

"Fine! Please, go ahead."

Even though I was still under a lot of stress, I was feeling a bit calmer listening to the monk's voice. He was not speaking in a normal tone, but his voice was gentle, like a melody that seemed to inspire a positive feeling of peace in my heart. Then, the monk started speaking:

"First, let me reassure you that you are totally safe here with us and that you can leave at any time you decide. I am Father Frankie, but you can call me Frank. I'm a monk and a traditional healer. But I am not the only one who has been treating you since we found you. The place you are now is a Holistic Health and Spiritual centre where people from different areas work together to do various healings as part of our social and spiritual volunteer work. Doctor Nick was the one who treated your wounds and provided you with first care when we found you, but there are a few other people involved in your healing. In this centre, we combine traditional western medicine with Reiki Energy Healing, Praying, Acupuncture and many creative expression techniques to provide holistic healing. Your case was especially difficult because you were seriously injured and seemed to have been through a lot. So, we sensed that you were in the need of help, and when we say help we don't mean only typical medical help. You were in the need of support. We know that you are here on a mission and we thought that it was not an accident that we found you.

"It's synchronicity!" I remarked, remembering my inner transformation moments on the plane to New York.

"Yes, it is synchronicity. You can give it any name you want. It doesn't matter." The monk said. "Names are pointers to something bigger than what words can sufficiently describe. You have to experience it in a way that it becomes a personal transformative experience."

"What else did you do to me?" I asked.

"Dr. Nick attended your wounds and gave your first care. Father Chris and I prayed for you and focused all our energy on your healing. Mark did acupuncture to you and Vivian and Harry did energy and spiritual healing while Mark did some kinesiotherapy to you. In addition, we all prayed together for you every day. Apparently it has worked. If you only had gone to the hospital, it might have taken many weeks for you to recover. You had a head injury, several broken bones, and your spine appeared injured as well. That's why I think we should all be happy and grateful that you have recovered so fast."

"Did you give me any pain killers?" I asked him, then.

"No, we didn't. We didn't give you any medication. We don't use pills in our treatments." The Monk said.

"Why not?" I asked him.

"Because we believe that pills are not fixing the problem. They just address and alleviate the symptoms while causing many side effects. In our centre, we believe that human body has a natural energy or life force that we can use to heal in the best way without chemicals. We can do that by relying on our body's natural intelligence and on the healing energies that are around us. We use our faith and the power of our mind, we try to connect to those higher energies available in the universe and attain physical, mental, emotional and spiritual healing. Eastern traditions, spiritual and religious schools have spoken about these forever. Modern science seems to confirm now that proper nutrition, positive thinking, praying, energy healing, acupuncture and others are the keys to healing and health and not the medication that cause side effects to our bodies leading to more damage than help."

"But this is how we treat diseases and help people here in the west, isn't it?" I asked the Monk.

"Yes. This is the way that the society had shaped us to believe that we are getting better. When what they seem to be doing is to inject chemicals into our bodies; chemicals that cause reactions and harm our organism. Did you know that more and more scientific studies seem to indicate that side effects of prescribed medication are the number one reason for death in the United States? Can you imagine that? The pills that the doctors prescribe to their patients with so much ease may have been the ones that cause the damage and lead to deaths. For us healers, pharmacies look like very unhealthy places. If you think about it, your system has been in a big crisis. But, there are so many studies explaining how healing occurs!"

"How does it occur?" I asked.

"Through our energy, our consciousness... Through thoughts, beliefs and emotions..."

"Can you explain more?"

"Do you feel the energy of your body?" Frank asked me.

"Sometimes." I replied.

"Have you ever tried to use it to feel better?"

I remembered then the breathing exercise I used to do to restore my balance and raise my energy, so I told him:

"Yes. I have done it sometimes."

"How have you done it?"

"I place my hands on my heart and basically take deep breaths, trying to relax."

"How did you end up doing that?"

"I don't know. Naturally, I guess."

"Exactly!" The monk exclaimed. "You were guided naturally to place your hands in your heart and try to restore your energy. What you were actually doing was to use the power of your intention in order to channel healing energies from the field or universe and clear negative blocks, energise your chakras and bring natural healing causing your body to change. Modern physics show us that our brains and body cells emit bio-photons, which are small emissions of light. With the power of our intention to heal, we can use bio-photons in order to affect and bring healing to the physical body. This is how healing occurs. They have found that praying works in the same way, also projecting energy from our minds and hearts when we concentrate and have the good intention to heal. Through love, we can affect matter in a significant way and perform miraculous healings."

"So you mean that just by wanting to get better and using our thoughts and emotions, we can heal more efficiently than taking pills?" I asked him.

"Yes, we do." He replied firmly.

"And why are doctors prescribing all those pills to us then? Why do we have so many pharmacies on every corner?"

"Money." The monk replied. "Money and a resistance to acknowledge that we humans are divine spiritual beings that have infinite abilities. That we can take charge of our health and healing. That we can create miracles in our daily life only through love, intention and awareness."

"Why am I still in bed then?" I asked.

"Because you have to cross this path by yourself. You can do it by believing on the power of your will and taking faith and personal responsibility for your health. And even though we have physically cured you, prayed for you, done energy healing, acupuncture, spiritual healing and other things, there is one thing that we can't do and that is up to you. There is one thing missing in order for you to get totally healed."

"What that would be?" I asked.

"This is something for you to discover." Said Frank, as he headed to the door. He came back holding a tray with a bowl of hot soup, fresh veggies, fruit and water in his hands.

"Eating natural food and drinking water is very important now for your healing." He told me, pointing to the tray.

I started eating and tried to see how my body was. It still didn't look good, but considering how badly hurt I had been, it really seemed a miracle that I was feeling so much better. I could be feeling much worse. At the same time, I felt very fascinated for all the things that Frank had told me and I wanted to know more.

"Can you tell me more about your process of healing?" I asked him.

"Yes, I can, but later... Now you need to rest and let your body do what it knows better. Tomorrow you can meet the rest of the team. As for now, you will allow me to go. I will pray for your recovering tonight before I sleep. If you need anything, please, ring this bell." The monk told me, pointing to a handmade bell sitting on the small desk behind my bed.

"Ok, I will." I said.

I was feeling tired and had doubts about the reality of what I was experiencing. I thought I might have been in a coma dreaming all of this. I decided to close my eyes and see if I would wake up in the same place the next day or if I had died and I was in a place that my imagination had created as a safe refuge. How can a spiritual place exist, where medical doctors, energy healers, acupuncturists, monks, priests, mediums and other people which believed in such different forms of healing coexist, work together and perform "miracles"? And why would they do that? I kept reflecting on all of this and trying to make some sense of it when I fell asleep.

I dreamed that night that I was in a different place. It was different than my usual dreams and my uncle was there sitting again and wearing white clothes. But this time, there were more people standing beside him that didn't look like normal human beings. They looked like angels. They were shining and radiating light. In my dream, I could see them, but I couldn't get close to them as I wasn't physically there. Still, it felt good.

# CHAPTER 8

## Meeting the rest of the cult – Awakening to the secrets of life

The following morning, I woke up feeling much better. My body didn't hurt so much and I thought I could try to walk. Before I tried to get out of bed the door opened and Frank entered the room.

"Good morning, Danny."

"Good morning."

"How do you feel today?"

"I feel much better and, as a matter of fact, I was thinking if I could try to stand up and walk."

"Look, you are doing much better and we think you will be able to go back home soon, but for the time being it may be better for you to rest more…"

"But, I don't want to go back home. I need to find my uncle. That's the reason I came here in the first place. That's why I'm in this position now. I gave the opportunity to those bastards to hurt me like that." I said, looking at the monk angrily.

"You seem to be angry, Danny, and you are losing your faith. You need to relax and transcend all the negative feelings, so you can help your body heal in the best way it knows. Our bodies work better when we have good feelings and emotions, when we engage in positive thinking. It is against nature to have negative feelings and most of them come from habitual thinking patterns. You need to accept what has happened to you and forgive those people that hurt you. Everything happens for a reason and we can grow if we learn to take our lessons and look on the positive side of all the things we experience, that's the way to freedom from external circumstances. That's the way to Nirvana or the Kingdom of Heaven as our fellow Christians call it, maintaining a pure heart, and keeping our faith levels up." The Monk said.

"What should I have faith in?" I asked him, then.

"You should first have faith in yourself; have faith that you are on an important mission here and that you are guided and assisted throughout all the way. The Universe is sending you signs all the time. God loves you. The only thing you have to do is to allow all this goodness to come to you."

"And how do you know that?"

"We know things here, Danny, the Monk told me looking into my eyes. We know because we take the time to pay attention and also we care about finding out. This is how we found you as well. Well... it wasn't really us, it was Tommy."

"Tommy? Who is Tommy?"

"Tom is not a registered part of our group, but he is helping us a lot with his acute senses and psychic abilities. Tommy is our cute cat. Jerry's cat. But let me tell you the whole story. We were doing a healing cycle when we all felt that something terrible was happening near here. It was probably the time you were attacked. Jerry had a strong feeling that there was a man in need and even said the first letter of your name. Tommy also started meowing in an unusual way and, then, we decided to go out and look for you. We were guided to the bar and it was Tommy that led us to the back where we found you on the floor unconscious. But don't worry, you will meet Tommy and Jerry soon. They will be here in a few minutes."

As I was listening to Father Frank talking with great attention and trying to process all the information, Jerry entered the room.

"Hello, Danny. It is so nice to meet you," he said.

I greeted him back. He went on:

"You look so much better!"

"So, are you the medium who saved my life?" I asked him emphatically.

"Yes, I am the one who felt your presence first. But as Frank should have already told you, it was actually Tommy who did the hard work. He's the one to thank for tracing you in that dark alley."

I asked him, then:

"Can you tell me where my uncle is?"

I thought that I should try my luck in case this entire story was real. If the guy was a medium with super abilities, he might be able to help me find my uncle. I immediately started hoping for the best again and believing in the inner and outer guidance I was receiving.

"Look, Danny, I will be very happy to help you find your uncle, but maybe you should rest a little more, so you are in a better state to do so.

"Ok!" I exclaimed. "I can do that."

I thought that since all these people were trying to help me and I was learning so many things at the same time, I could be patient and stay there a little longer so I could recover, build up my energy and, then, continue the search for my uncle.

I stayed there for a few days talking to them about my life, my work, my friends, my wife Rosa and our kids, my father and my journey to New York. I also recounted with every detail the transformational moments I went through in the plane and my changes and realisations. They all listened with great attention and told me many amazing stories of healing and miracles that they have witnessed while they were working in the spiritual centre. I was totally amazed about all the things I was learning. It was a soul enhancing experience that was widening my reality and my view of the cosmos.

One morning, Jerry and Frank came in and asked me if I wanted to go to the praying room to pray with them. I agreed and tried to get up. Doctor Nick helped me to walk to the praying room. It was quite hard to walk and I felt lots of pain, but I tried to hang on. When I entered the room I saw the images in the wall. There was a huge image of Jesus, one of Mother Teresa, several statues of Buddha and other Spiritual and Religious symbols and images. The place was an amalgam of spirituality, religion, tradition and healing. I started thinking then that if a place like that existed, anything could be possible in this world. The whole group was already there waiting for the rest of us. After a few minutes looking around the room, they helped me to sit down and we started praying.

The energy of the place was amazing. I immediately felt much better only by being there. I felt a warm wave of energy, love, and peace entering my heart. I felt that only by being there I was receiving healing in every possible way. I felt my body becoming much lighter and my energy raising. I closed my eyes and tried to breathe deeply and relax even more. I wasn't sure of how to pray, but I took a few deep breaths and tried to relax and connect more to the place. I also tried to connect to my heart and channel as much energy as I could through deep conscious breathing. I immediately felt part of a whole. I felt connected. I felt I belonged. I understood I am an integral part of this Universe. I thought of my uncle, then, who said the same words in his letter. I immediately understood that the entire world is God's nest. My uncle was not speaking literally. He probably had some similar spiritual experience of deep connection and he felt the same connectedness and belonging. I was tuning into the same feeling at that particular moment, in God's nest. I felt that God exists everywhere. So this feeling of divine grace can be accessed from anywhere, as long as the right conditions and state of mind exist. The right conditions seemed to exist in that unique place where various people that appeared different seemed to connect and work together, sharing the same values and will, to help others and evolve. Compassion was the reason they were doing it. I could feel it clearly at this point. The more I was sinking deeper into that inner state, the more peacefully I felt, and the more my heart was filled with love and compassion. I was feeling my body dissolving and my soul emanating and connecting to the universal soul of heart, love and compassion. At that point, I knew that time and space didn't matter. I knew that everything is perfect the way it is. I knew that I was making my life hard by not being aware of that feeling of bliss, by not having a kind, open and compassionate heart.

I stayed there feeling divine grace until a bell rung and Frank stood up. He asked if anyone wanted to speak about his/her experience. Miraculously, I managed to stand up without help and started talking:

"First, I would like to thank you all for everything you did for me, you saved my life, but more importantly you showed a different reality to me, a different path for my soul. Frank's teachings and the feelings of presence, kindness, servitude and compassion that you all share here made me awaken to the truths of our existence. I understand now that we are not only weak bodies moving aimlessly around ourselves. We are immortal souls having an opportunity to make our life matter. We can make the difference. I promise that I will try to hold onto this realisation and live the rest of my life with love and compassion, with trust and awareness. I will try to live a "God realised life", helping others to feel the same way.

When I finished with my short talk, Father Chris stood up again and said a short prayer of Gratitude and Compassion for the whole world, then they all came to me and wished me a quick recovery and safe return home. I walked back to the room on my own feeling much better. I was totally amazed by the miracle happening in front of my eyes. I could never imagine that my quest to find my uncle would lead me to discover my higher self, feel divine grace and connect to the universal Soul of God, the real God, the one of love, compassion, peace and kindness, not the one they manufacture in the various religious institutions and sell ruthlessly across the globe. I had awakened to the power of my own existence. My faith was restored.

When I returned to my room a tray with fresh veggies, fruits and a glass of fresh orange juice were waiting for me. All the people were also gathered there. They asked me what I would do next. I told them that I would find my uncle and go home. I didn't know how, but I knew I would meet him very soon. I also missed Rosa and my kids. I couldn't wait to go back home and give them a big hug. I was feeling that my life had meaning because I loved them and I could put them all above my little self. I knew that this whole quest was meant to mature me in a way that I could go back and offer them my unconditional love. I could also live my life from a very different perspective. I could try to align my personal and social life with my realisations. I could be a new man living in a new Earth.

# Chapter 9

## Message from my uncle

When I woke up in the following morning, I was feeling ready to go. I had no dreams during the previous night. I just felt I was cured. I had breakfast with Frank and the rest of the people. I met Tommy and gave him some cuddles and pats to share my love and affection. I had a shower, thanked everyone and got into a taxi that would drive me back to the hotel. They insisted that I should go to the hospital for a check up, but I was convinced that it wasn't necessary. Nature healing has taken its course in a miraculous way.

When I went back to the hotel, I had decided that I wouldn't try to find my uncle any more. I knew that when the time was right, he would find me. I decided to pack my things and fly back to Sydney. I had gotten all the answers I needed and I was sure that the destabilising dreams would stop. After I packed my things, I went down to the reception to check out. I wasn't stressed out anymore, or lost in my thoughts. I was relaxed and peaceful. I was feeling good. I couldn't wait to go back to my old life as my new self. I knew that my change of view of myself and the world would make the difference. I knew that if I applied all these teachings to my life, it would make the difference for me, my family and the rest of the world.

When I asked the guy in the reception if I was ready to check out, he said "yes" and handed me my ID. Then, while I was walking to the door, he called me back:

"Well, Sir, excuse me… Actually, there is something else."

"What would that be?" I asked him.

"There was a man looking for you the other day as soon as you left the hotel, but we thought we shouldn't bother you with that."

"What man?" I asked. "What are you talking about?"

"Well, there was a homeless man saying that he is your uncle and that he needed to find you because you were in danger. We thought he was crazy and that we shouldn't bother you with that."

"Oh my God!" I exclaimed. "This is not possible. Did he leave any message for me?"

"Well, yes. He said that he will wait for you in God's nest." The reception guy said.

"Did he say when?" I asked.

"No, he didn't."

"Did he say anything else?"

"No, we weren't sure if he was telling the truth, so we didn't talk to him a lot."

I thought that I should go back to the pub and try to find my uncle there. He would have probably talked to the people in God's Nest leaving directions for me on how to find him. On the other hand, I started reflecting on all of my spiritual experiences and the realisations I had in the spiritual centre and my decision to go back home. I felt confused. My energy dropped. I was in a dilemma. I looked at the guy and told him that I would stay in the hotel for a little longer. I decided to stay for one more night and give it a last go. I knew that despite my realisations and transformation my uncle still had something to do with all of this. I felt that he held important information for me. I also realised how foolish I was when I was thinking before that I would save my uncle when I was the one who needed to be saved. I asked the staff in the reception to take my luggage back to the room and I called for a taxi. I would go back to God's Nest.

I entered the taxi and said hello.

"You don't seem to be from here." The taxi driver told me.

"No, I am not." I replied.

"And where are you from?" If I may ask.

"I'm from Sydney." I replied.

"Sydney? Australia!" He exclaimed. "It can't be!"

"Why not?"

"You know... My brother lives there..."

"Oh nice!" I said. "Where about?"

"In Sydney!"

"Have you ever been there?"

"No, never." He said. "But I would love to... Maybe one day... Who knows..."

"Well, since your brother is there, you can stay at his place, if you decide to go... Right?".

He replied:

"Well, the truth is that I don't think I can stay at my brother's house."

"Why not?" I asked.

"Because he doesn't have one."

"Is your brother...?" I started asking and then paused for a moment.

He, then, told me:

"He is homeless, yeah..."

"Wow! I can't believe that." I said.

"Why not?"

"It is a long story. Tell me about your brother. How long has he been in the streets?"

"He has been there for the last 20 years..."

"20 years??"

"Yes!"

"And why is that, if I may ask?"

"Well, he told us when he decided to leave that he couldn't stay here anymore. He couldn't stay in a country where his ancestors were slaves and symbolic slavery still prevails. He didn't want to pay taxes to a government like that and to avoid civil disobedience, he just left..."

"So, he decided to go to Australia? Didn't he know about the Aboriginals and the stolen generations there?"

"Yes, he did. But he thought he would give it a go and see how he would feel. He didn't have many options anyway. You see my brother had asthma and the doctors advised him to move to a place with a warmer climate and as he spoke the language and Australia is warm he decided to go there."

I then asked:

"So, it wasn't merely because of political convictions, was it?"

"To tell you the truth, I have been thinking about myself. The thing is that when we are young we have ambitions and values. We have a pure heart. When we become adults, we start to forget all of this and get attached to material things. We ignore our dreams and our values suppressing them into our unconscious. Most of the people end up living an unconscious life and become depressed or sick. Then their unconscious often awakens and comes into consciousness reminding them about all these dreams and values they had. It's hard. Trust me. The game of socialisation is a hard game that only a very few people, if any, know how to play. I guess my brother was fighting with all of this when he made the decision."

I, then, told him:

"You are right and without meaning to offend you, from the way you talk, you seem more like an academic than a taxi driver."

He replied:

"I haven't driven a taxi for all my life. I used to teach sociology at a University."

"What happened then?"

"Shit happened. While I was getting to know more and more about society, studying about the psyche and human behaviour, identity and consciousness, my mother started suffering from bipolar disorder and committed suicide. My sister started taking sleeping pills and, then, became a drug addict. And my brother went to Australia and became homeless. So I thought if I couldn't help the people I love, my own family, what was the purpose of me teaching in a University about these things?"

"But, there is a purpose!" I told him firmly. "You need to help people that will cross your path and are willing to listen to you. You also need to be a positive example. You can't save anyone because everyone has to go through their own life experiences so they can grow and mature spiritually. Sometimes it seems easier to help strangers, people that you don't know, than your own family. Our families know us in a very different way and it is hard to make them listen to us and accept our help. They always see us in a different way. At the same time, we can always try to help them by sending them positive energy. Of course, we can't do everything for them. As I said, everyone has to learn their own way and rhythm. That is obvious, don't you think?" I asked him firmly.

"I do know it." He replied. "I guess I got desperate. I had issues dealing with all the things that were happening at my home and I was too proud to ask for help. My ego was too strong. What would people think?"

I then asked:

"You felt both disappointed and ashamed?"

"Yes, I did." He said.

"To be honest with you, I think that you studied all of your life to become a Professor of Sociology and it should be for a reason. You probably have a mission to accomplish, a destiny, a dharma… And you didn't…Don't you think about that? .

"Of course I do. You are not the only one I met who is reminding me about this. I came across many cases where I had to reflect on what has happened to me. I had to live it over and over again. You can't imagine how it is. All these coincidences pointing to the same thing…"

"Let me ask you… What advice would you give to yourself?"

"To go through counselling perhaps. Deal with my past and release the painful memories. Then, I could perhaps go on with my life. I could either keep driving the taxi or even change profession, perhaps going back to my academic research and work at Uni. It wouldn't matter though since the past wouldn't haunt me anymore."

"That's exactly what you have to do: deal with your past, accept it, release emotions and let it go… Then you can move on… I, then, put my hand in his pocket and gave him a piece of paper.

"What is that?" He asked me.

"It is a spiritual centre I stayed at for a couple of days. You may want to go to there. They can help you a lot. Tell them that Danny sent you… Tell them it is synchronicity… They will understand. They are probably waiting for you already."

He asked:

"Who are they?"

"They are good people, nice people, compassionate. They will help you."

"Ok! Thank you." Said the taxi driver who for some reason seemed to trust me enough to follow this advice. He didn't want to accept money for the ride, but I insisted on paying him. I told him to take care and I got out of the taxi. We were at God's Nest.

# CHAPTER 10

## Keeping the faith and listening to my inner voice

I entered the pub. It had more people this time. I started looking around in case I recognised my uncle. He didn't seem to be there. I went straight to the bar and looked for the bartender. He was not there either. I asked the bartender, then, about John's whereabouts. He told me that John quitted his job. I asked him why. He said that he went back to Uni. I guess that was good news for John, but not for me. I needed information.

"Has a homeless man with the name Tom left any information for me?" I asked the new bartender, then, and continued: "My name is Danny by the way."

"And I'm Peter. Who are you looking for?"

"I am looking for my uncle Tom. He left home many years ago to live in the streets. I think he tried to communicate with me through my dreams."

I didn't know why I was passing on all of this information and trusting this guy, but I had a hunch that I should.

"Interesting," said Peter. "So, your uncle is homeless?"

"Yes, I guess he is." I replied and went on: "Do you know him?"

"No I don't. We have a few homeless people living around here and they, sometimes, come here to help, as John would have probably told you, I guess."

"Yes I know. John actually brought me into contact with a couple of them and I talked to a homeless man named Peter a few days ago."

"And what did he say to you?"

"He told me to wait for my uncle to contact me first, but I don't live around here. I came all the way from Sydney, Australia. I had to leave my work and family to come here so I can't just sit around and do nothing, waiting for my uncle. Peter said that if my uncle had such abilities to communicate with me through my dreams, then he should be on top of the process. Peter , then, asked me what had brought me to God's Nest and I explained that my uncle sent us a letter a few years ago, mentioning the name of the pub at the end of his letter. His words seemed poetic and symbolic, but I though the name could be real."

"Hmm I see... Can I see the letter?"

"Yes, sure."

"Sorry for asking you that, but you made me really curious now." Said the bartender with a smile in his face.

I gave him the letter and he started reading it.

"Interesting! It's a long shot, but you may have a point here..."

"Can you see something else?" I asked him.

"Well, your uncle seems to mention water and it rains a lot here indeed. He also speaks about the beach."

"The beach?"

"Yeah! How he enters the water at the beach and feels nice and all... Did you try to go to the beach?"

"Which beach? Is there one close here?" I asked.

"Yes, there is. It's half an hour drive north. Do you have a car?"

"No, I don't..."

"I would offer you a ride, but my car broke down and it won't be ready for a couple of days."

"It's ok.I will find a way to get there. Thank you so much." I replied.

"No need to thank me, my friend. I am always happy to help. Do you know how many people have come here day and night telling me about the stories of their lives? I should write a book one day."

"Sounds like a good idea." I said to him and left the bar.

I got into a taxi and went back to the hotel. I knew it was a long shot to go to the beach, but I didn't have any other choice. I had to take my chances with that. I was trying to convince myself that I was still on track. I had to think positive and keep up my faith. I slept for a few hours that night and I had a very nice dream. I saw myself sitting on the sand by the beach, feeling my body lighter and floating. In the following morning, I woke up with a warm feeling in my heart. I thought that my emotional world was being restored. How could it not be? I had come to learn so many things during my quest. I just had to find my uncle now, so I could solve the mystery and go back home. I decided to have a quick shower and a light breakfast at the hotel. I had also come to realise that the lighter and more natural my food was, the more energy I would get. Everything has importance in life. Our life is not to be lived randomly. There is meaning and I was finding it.

After I finished showering I called for a taxi. They said it would arrive in five minutes. I put some clothes on and went down to the waiting room.

The taxi arrived at the hotel. I got onto the taxi and asked the driver to take me to Gold Star beach. He started driving and then, on the radio, a reporter started talking about a robbery at a bank which resulted in the brutal death of two guards. The driver turned up the volume to listen to it better.

"Can you please change station on the radio?" I politely asked the driver who seemed to be very surprised with my request. I kept saying: "Will you excuse me for asking, but I have been through a lot lately and I can't bear hearing any bad news."

He replied:

"I understand."

"It's amazing how TV and radio bombard us with all these negative events every day, isn't it?" I remarked.

The driver agreed.

"They try to convince us by constant repetition that all these horrible things happening everyday are natural, when they aren't." I added.

The driver said:

"Yeah, they do. I don't even want to think how much garbage I have swallowed from the media in the past. Watching the news is like watching soap operas. They focus on money, accidents, disasters plus all these advertisement products promoting capitalism and a shallow life based on material pleasure. They brainwash us in so many ways that we can't even imagine. I've just remembered about an article I read some years ago by a psychiatrist explaining the harmful effects of TV, not only through the content but also as a medium. The article was describing how our brain waves extend from our brains and connect to the various electronic devices creating a system where humans and machines become one, exchanging information and genes. I thought it is amazing how television harm us in so many different ways. I decided to stop watching TV at home. What a waste of time when there are so many others things we can do in our free time, such as looking at this amazing view I had from the window of the taxi while driving to the beach."

We were crossing a large road with tall trees and lots of beautiful flowers on the sidewalk. It was a sunny day, a perfect day.

The taxi driver began to relax and appeared to start enjoying the ride. Soon enough we arrived at the beach. I paid the driver, thanked him for the ride and wished him a nice day.

# CHAPTER 11

# Magical moments at the beach

When I arrived at the beach I was amazed. It was a very beautiful natural environment. I immediately took my shoes off and started walking on the sand. The beach was empty, I guess because it was early and most people would be working. The water was magical. There were no waves and the sun light were mirroring on the sea, creating a bright spectrum of gold light. I walked for a while by the sea and, then, laid still on the sand. I closed my eyes and started taking deep breaths. I felt peaceful. It seemed as if all my problems, stress, concerns didn't follow me to the beach. They stayed behind. My dream from the previous night had come true. I was experiencing the same heavenly feeling. For a moment, I stopped worrying about finding my uncle or about my life's purpose. I thought that our life purpose should be to find peace, to be able to enjoy a day at the beach under the sun. I realised that we don't need many things in life in order to be happy, but unfortunately we deceive ourselves to believe that we do. In the process of socialisation, we get attached to our material possessions, get too busy pursuing our egoistic ambitions and end up missing out on life itself. We end up missing out on those magical moments, the simple things that life can offer like the sun, the beach, the sand, the water, the ability to close our eyes and just let go of everything, being able to relax.

I felt I belonged there. I felt connected. I felt that I found the meaning of life. Like wise men used to say "Beauty in its simplicity". I had left so much beauty behind in Sydney to come all the way here. I had left my beautiful wife, my children, my family, my friends, my house, my garden, even my work. I was sure now that I could go back and look at the positive side of all things. I could shift my mentality at work, so I could help people connect to their inner wisdom instead of just trying to make money for the company I worked for. I could even quit that job and open my own office or try to do some voluntary work. It was up to me. I could choose. I could even start doing something new. I know now that I could. We could and should be the directors and protagonists of our own lives and blame no one for our misfortunes.

Everything happens for a reason. There was a reason for everything that happened in my life so far. There was a meaning. The only difference is the degree of realisation. I couldn't realise it before. I needed to leave all of my social life behind for a while and embark on a crazy trip in order to learn and grow. My trip was successful after all. Regardless of finding my uncle or not, I have found my true self, but "where is my uncle?" I thought for a moment. He should be around. I opened my eyes again and looked around. I had a strong feeling that my uncle was close. I could sense his presence, a calling. I wonder why... How come my uncle is homeless and could do all these things? Or was it my imagination? Did I go after a homeless man because I wasn't happy with my life and needed some adventure? What about my dreams? I was trying to understand... I felt my energy dropping, then, and I closed my eyes again and started taking deep breaths. What an amazing feeling!

I wondered if going for a walk in the park, by the beach or in any other natural environment, or for a swim could help people who take sleeping pills, antidepressants and need distractions all day long in order to feel better? Why can't everyone appreciate nature? Why couldn't I have appreciated nature before? It is evident that beauty is out there all the time. Answers are there too. Guidance. It is us who need to open our eyes and recognise the beauty, see the signs, hear the answers. It's not the world that is wrong. It's our perception of the world. We see world as an unfriendly battlefield. We think that we only need to look after our own little selves in order to survive when this is not the only way. I could see clearly now that it's all in our mind. I was awakening to our unlimited potential. I was changing the way I saw myself. I started to come present and notice the beauty all around, I was finding meaning.

Meaning exists in the simple things of life, in nature, in kindness and compassion, in communication, in servitude... Meaning cannot be found in ambitious pursuits, egoistic lives, stress, worries and fears. Fear is killing us. It is stopping our growth. And most of the things we fear come from conditioning, from the brainwashing of the media, from our own families and society, from our teachers and culture. During my trip, I met people from different cultures going beyond that, beyond their doctrines and working together to help others in need. I met people like taxi drivers and bartenders caring enough to listen and help. I saw miracles happening when people want to help, when they are kind. I saw kindness and compassion, love as the source of life, the motivating force of the Universe. This feeling of love is what creates everything in life. Healings are communicated with love. Families are created with love. God is love. The Universe is moved by love. Whatever the question is, the answer is love.

I realised at that moment that I had not loved myself before, that I hadn't even known my real self. I had stopped listening to my heart and ended up being at the wrong place at the wrong time. Real communication with loved ones happens only with love and how can we communicate with others if we don't first communicate with ourselves, if we don't love ourselves? I realised at that moment that it is ok to love myself. It is ok to seek happiness and meaning. And it doesn't take a lot to have that. Just some self-respect, honesty, kindness and awakening to the lies and truths of our existence. Some of them, I was blessed to discover during my trip. It was both an inner and outer journey where I connected to my heart and my true self. I started paying attention to life's small details, to awaken to all the things around me, to see the beauty, to taste my food, to smell the roses, to feel my heart, to feel nice. It doesn't take much. It only takes presence, intention, love, awareness, kindness and compassion. They are just words, but they point to states that can save the world. We have to save ourselves first and then try to save the world and this is what I did on my journey. I saved myself, my real self, while the fake one with all the additional layers

I have created was breaking apart. All these layers that added suffering to my life and distracted me from the important things in life had started to fall apart. I was ascending. I realised that I am a spiritual being primarily, a soul, a spirit, a heart, a consciousness and, then, all the rest. I realised that my name, profession and social roles do not have to define me. I can still participate in various social events while remembering who I really am. I could still have various relationships with all sort of people without expecting them to define me, approve me or make me feel important. I realised that the opinions of others about me is none of my business. And why should they be? As a spirit, I was already perfect. We all are! We need no more. I could still have a house, clothes, money and material possessions, but they didn't have to define me. I didn't have to be attached to them, trying to find meaning through them and asking for more. We can't find meaning in money and fame. They are only means that can be seen in a symbolic way as offering abundance and opportunities to grow more. We can find temporal pleasure and 'self' assurance in material possessions but not real meaning. Real meaning is found when we encounter the world with respect, with kindness, with love, with a pure heart and a clear mind. Then, we gain peace of mind regardless of our external circumstances. My values have changed in a few days from career and money to spirituality, love and peace of mind, God's will... I was awakening to my true existence, to my divine self, the one we all have within. I saw reality from a different angle and I knew how I should live my life from now on, with love.

It was then that the sound of a cane interrupted my delirium of feelings and realisations. I opened my eyes to see an old man, walking by the beach, he seemed weak and his cane was cutting the sand, appearing as it would open the earth in two. I felt an intense feeling while I was looking at this man, who stopped walking, then, and looked at me.

-"Danny," he called my name. "Stand up! It's me, your uncle Tom."

# CHAPTER 12

# Meeting my uncle in God's nest

I was amazed to hear my uncle calling my name. I couldn't believe he was there. I stood up and started walking towards him.

-"Hello, Danny! How do you feel?"

"I feel good."

"Are you enjoying your day at the beach?"

"Yeah. I am."

"How's your life in the streets?" I asked abruptly.

"Life in the streets is like life at any place Danny, sometimes it is good, sometimes bad."

"But it's harder here, isn't it?"

"It depends. Well, to be honest, yes! At the beginning it was harder, much harder, but I think that your life is not easy either, is it? I'm sure you know better now, don't you?"

-"Yes, I do! But I still can't understand how someone would leave the comfort of his house and family, having a hot shower and an easy meal in order to live a hard life on the streets."

"Maybe because this home, family, shower and meal come with a price Danny, a price that was too high for me to pay... Do you know how many people live in the streets by choice?"

"Yes. I have heard of many. You are one of them, right?"

-"Yes, I am! I took a choice. What about you Danny? Have you chosen to live a socialised life or have you had no choice?"

"Why would I need to choose that when it was given to me?"

"It was given to you together with so many other things, right?"

"Yes, I guess so..."

"So, tell me the real reason you came all the way here... Is it to confront me about my choice to live in the streets?"

"Maybe it is... To tell you the truth, I haven't understood the reason yet. I just knew I should find you and talk to you."

"Was it because of your dreams?"

"How do you know about my dreams? Did you try to contact me through my dreams?"

"No, I think you did. Your unconscious was so desperate and tried to find a way to rescue your consciousness."

"What are you talking about? I had everything back there, I needed no more. Now I know that. I realised that. I just needed to change the way I see my life and my life would change."

"And did you? Did you change that?"

"Yes, I think I did. I am trying..."

"You are trying... Come on Danny, you have to be more confident than that. Following all your realisations... You should be talking more firmly. You have to own your realisations and know how to use them in every aspect of your life."

"How do you know about all of this? Are you some kind of medium or psychic?"

"Well, I do know things. You know Danny, leaving behind society and leaving everything behind, you start to see life differently; you change. Life in the streets is not easy. You can't go around distracted, stressed, lost in your mind... You wouldn't survive like that. You have to be alert, use all your senses. You have to be present. Then slowly you start to know more, to feel things, to get a feeling. You know, Danny, that the present moment hides all the information we need for the future. You can observe only in the present moment the patterns that reveal what might happen. You can see the Karma, you can "read" someone or something. Let me tell you something...

Do you know, Danny, that I felt closer to your father and society and everyone when I went away than when I was physically close to them? You know that I could sense the bonds, these invisible connections of love that exist between people who cared for each other. I could really see love. I experienced all these feelings that I couldn't experience before. My heart was cold back there and I was cut off from my feelings. I had to go. My life was not good. I couldn't find a way out. I guess you had a similar experience in your small trip, didn't you? You saw things differently too and realised many things."

"Yes, I did. But still, I wouldn't go to live in the streets. I can't understand that..."

"You can't understand because you are not ready to let go of everything, are you?"

"And why should I be? Why did you do it?"

"Because I couldn't live any more the way I was. I felt more and more distant from myself and all others. I felt like a robot, an automaton, a caricature..."

"Does this feeling remind you of something Danny?"

"Yeah, it does. But... When you came here and realised all of this, why didn't you want to go back, then?"

"Because I was afraid."

"Afraid of what?"

"Of forgetting. I was afraid that if I went back, I would be doing the same things, missing out on life, feeling distant, not living life, not feeling the love, the connection, the belonging... On the other hand, I got so involved here with the homeless community that I couldn't leave them behind anymore. They needed me and I needed them."

"And you decided to stay with them and pay such a price?"

"Yes, I did. But talking about prices, what is the price you had to pay to live the life you used to live?"

"It was a big one."

"What was it?"

"My real self, my life, my peace of mind, this love, the connectedness, the divine grace I felt on the plane, the compassion I felt at the spiritual centre, the enlightenment I felt at the beach. But I have the feeling that you already know about all of these, don't you?"

"Yes, I do! More or less…"

"Now, tell me this Danny, did you meet Frank?"

"Yes, I did."

"Do you know him?"

"Yes, I do. We have worked together in various "projects" for the homeless community. We worked together with simple things like constructing shelters from plastic paper and tree leaves to bigger things like past life healings and all sorts of spiritual work."

"And why Father Frank didn't tell me about you? I can't believe that…"

"I guess because he knew that it was not the time yet…"

"Where do you live? I had so many questions on my mind that I wanted to ask you…"

"I live in God's nest! Daniel, it's not the place you have visited so many times, that pub. It is here, this beach, the river further away, the tree on the other side of the city, the lakes, the rocks, it is everywhere… It is nature. This is God's nest."

"What about the pub? Was that a coincidence?"

"All coincidences have meaning in life, Danny. You should know that very well by now. Nothing is accidental. In every random place hides a big truth. Experts call it serendipity. In the streets, we call it 'just look'. You can see we avoid fancy names here. We call the synchronicities "look-better". We call energy healing "love touch". We like our language to be simpler, so all the people can understand it. Danny, tell me now, what have you learned so far?"

While I was talking to my uncle, I was feeling better and better, more relaxed. I really felt close to him, but not as an old family member… More as a soul mate, a kind spirit that had decided to be more honest with life and himself and grow spiritually in this life. I started telling him about all my realisations, about the plane and the synchronicities I experienced, about the healing water, the magic soup, the energy healing, the praying and the transformational moments in the spiritual centre, the energy of nature, what I have learned about pills and traditional medicine, the compassion, love, our unlimited potential, the inner and outer guidance I was receiving. I recounted everything with every small detail. My uncle seemed very fascinated to hear all of this. His look appeared to validate all my realisations.

"And how do you feel after experiencing all these quantum moments or epiphanies as they call them?" My uncle asked me.

"I feel great. I feel reborn. I feel that I have found my true self, that I discovered the true meaning of life. I just wish I could go back home and hug Rosa and my kids. I also wish I could make my father feel better about you and everything that happened in the past. I wish I could."

"You wish you could save the world, don't you?"

"Yes I do, but I feel I can't."

"Well I felt the same. It's ok. We can't save the world, Daniel. We can only save ourselves so we can be an example of Pure Positive Energy. I'm sure you realised that too, didn't you?

"Yes, I did. I just have to accept it. Acceptance and awareness are the keys to gain peace of mind! Accept things the way they are unconditionally and be grateful for them. That is true love."

"And this is what you are after now, isn't it?"

"Yes, it is."

My uncle seemed to know everything. He seemed to know better. My whole idea of homeless people being crazy was changing. My uncle was not crazy. He was extremely nice and wise. He was very honest and sensitive.

"And how do you hide your sensitivity in the streets?" I asked him.

"I don't. Here in the streets, I can express it in the best ways. Can you imagine how many people are in real need here and they don't have an ego preventing them to ask for help. I can help them and by helping them, I am also helping myself, I'm saving myself."

"It seems as if a monk or a priest is speaking."

My uncle laughed.

"It is funny, Danny, how people think about God. They think God belongs to the church, to few special people. God is everywhere and in everything, in every one of us. He doesn't discriminate. God is just not with a priest, or a monk and less with a homeless. He is everywhere. He is with everyone. It's the degree of realisation and allowing that varies. As long as you realise that God is here with you and you allow His presence, then you don't have to be a monk, or a priest to contact Him and feel the divine grace. You just have to be nice, keep an open heart and seek contact. God comes to the open hearts, the clear from distractions, from passions, from bad thoughts, to those who allow Him."

"Is there something you want me to tell dad back home?"

"Just tell him that I'm fine and I love him. I'm closer to him than before and thank him for all the time he has spent thinking of me and feeling sorry. Tell him that it is ok. I am fine. He doesn't need to worry about me. I know he still does. He doesn't have to save me."

"But you can save him, right?"

"No, I can't. Everyone has to save themselves, Danny. We can just help."

"Help?"

"Yes. Help!"

"How?"

"...With a kind word, a good deed, a nice thought, an honest smile, a tap on the shoulder, pointing a sign, telling our story, by connecting to them in a soul level with honesty and a smile, by listening empathetically to what they have to say, by accepting them unconditionally or by being warm and genuine and compassionate. You know now all of this, don't you?"

"Yes, I do!"

"Is there anything else you would like to talk about?"

"No, I don't think there is! I am ready to go back to Rosa and my kids now...back to society. I want to try to make some difference..."

"Yes, I think you will! Thank you for coming to see me."

"I thank you."

I hugged my uncle and started walking away. Before I hit the road, my uncle shouted from the back,:

"Oh and Daniel, I forgot to tell you... Don't be afraid, you are not going to die!"

I turned his head back and looked bedazzled at my uncle.

"What do you mean?" I shouted.

"You will discover soon." My uncle replied.

For some strange reason, I started to believe as well that I wouldn't die like my uncle told me. I guess my life had changed so much over the last days in a way that it made me understand that nothing is random and that there is a deeper purpose, a higher organising intelligence, offering us guidance and signs; and that there may be also another "side" where we go to when we leave our physical body...

I was saying that to myself and at the same time getting more and more scared as I thought that I may actually die one day soon and it may be the end...

I started questioning everything again. I didn't know what was happening. What was real and what was not... if I was just being paranoid going after my uncle and believing in all this stuff or if I was finding my real self... Not dying? I thought... Have I discovered all the truths I was looking for, after all, or are there more?? What is the meaning of all of this? How could that be?

Well maybe I should just wait and see. Maybe I should have faith indeed. Maybe God has a bigger plan for me, far more wonderful and divine than I expected. Maybe I should just let go of all my fear and attempt to control everything and start trusting the process more... I guess maybe the universe wants to test me in ways that will prove my faith and test my increased consciousness and perception... Who knows maybe there is another side and it will be nice over there... on the other side... and the more I am thinking about it, the more I realise that there should be another side! Now, I am feeling more and more certain! Now, I believe... I can feel it... We can't just die and that's it. That can't be the end... What is the purpose of just coming into this physical manifestation, moving from here to there, creating, destroying, growing, fading out and then dying? It doesn't seem right. There should be something more than that. All these spiritual experiences I was having on my journey clearly point to the fact that there should be another dimension; that of the spirit world where we all come from and we all end up after a small physical journey. I guess our mission on earth should be to learn, grow and mature spiritually, to learn in a deep soul level, love, create and remember where we came from and who we really are. Then, we return to that place where we can again join our Source, join God, becoming one with the divine consciousness, with the source of creation where everything comes from and ends up, where everything begins and finishes and starts again…

Immediately, I started wondering what could be in the other side… How would things be there? What kind of body would we end up with? Would we be just a stream of light, an energy body, a lighter vibration, a spirit, soul or third eye, or something else, something more or something less, something that we can't even begin to imagine now while in our physical body, in our earthly vehicle?

I suddenly started to appreciate my body more and think that I should have taken better care of it. Our body is our temple, our earthly vehicle that allows us to move and do all the things that we came here to do. Our body is a present, a sacred space. Let's say that we are endowed so we can move through this physical experience and yet most of the people don't care about their body; they don't give it the right food and they don't take regular exercise. They don't get enough rest and they don't appreciate it and love it, accept it and honour it, connect to it and travel within, speak to its parts and feel its vast energy and endless depths, its vast space that lies within, a hidden universe, an endless space that modern science keeps discovering and in which it travels deeper and deeper.

There is a double way happening, one out there to the space, exploring distant galaxies and stars and one within our human body, to our cells and even deeper discovering the zero point field, the black whole… The scientists keep moving deeper within and further out there… and the more depths they reach, the more they realise that there is much more to go. The absolute, the infinite both out there and within…

I kept thinking while walking on the road leading far away from the beach, waiting for a taxi or a car to pick me up… Unfortunately there was nothing there so I kept walking and walking sunk in my thoughts…

Suddenly a taxi appeared. I raised my hand and waved at the taxi which stopped a few meters away. I then ran to the taxi and asked the driver for a ride. I went back to the hotel, packed my things and went to the airport. I wanted to catch the late flight that night to go back to Sydney, go back to my wife and kids and to my new life.

When I was in the plane, I was thinking how hard it was to believe all the things that I had experienced in this journey. I managed to find my uncle, but more than that I managed to find my real self. I discovered my mission in this world. If I could make a significant impact on the life of the people I met just by talking honestly to them and telling my story, then imagine what I could do if I started devoting my life to that. This is my mission in the world to share my story with other people and help them connect with their higher selves. I need also to remember to stay present in the process reading the signs the universe is sending me and appreciating life in its fullness. I am not sure if I will die or not as my uncle told me, if this plane will crash or if I will manage to get back to my home. What matters is that I can now change my Karma and create the life I want and maybe help other people do the same. I can become a Coach, a Counsellor, a Spiritual teacher or an inspirational writer and try to make the world a better place. So far, I had been using my talents in the courtrooms winning cases and making money for my company. Now, it is the time to go back and use my talents to help other people awaken to their true potential and gain enlightenment.

Everyone thought I was a fool when I decided to risk everything and embark on this journey, but by trusting my intuition and following the signs, I managed to find my real self and now I am going back home as a whole person. I can look Rosa in the eyes now and hug my kids knowing who I am. I don't have to hide behind my title, my material possessions, my name and my ambitions. Now I know that I am something bigger than all of that. I don't have to define my identity from those things. Jesus said that: *"I am the son of God and you are the son of God"*. Now, I know that I am divine. I discovered that higher part within me that is superior from any of the problems that I used to have when I was in Sydney. I can still be Danny, a husband, a father, a son and even a lawyer, but I don't have to define my identity from these and get lost in these various roles. Now I know that I am a superior spiritual being that has a big mission in life. I also know that you, who is reading these lines now, are a superior spiritual being too and in case I won't meet you in person in Australia, Greece, Brazil or anywhere else around the world to tell you that, I would like to pass this message to you now through this book.

Take the power that belongs to you back to your hands.

Take a good look within and decide what you really want in your life.

Start trusting your intuition and do whatever it takes to discover your mission.

Have faith in your success.

Express your unique talents creatively and offer your gifts to the world with unconditional love.

It is not so much the destination that matters. What really matter is the trip.

Enjoy the trip and remember also to stop and smell the flowers.

You are present, you are divine, you are unique.

God loves you.

Do you love yourself?

# Epilogue

As already mentioned in the preface, when I started writing this novel I didn't have a clue about how the story would unfold or end. It was a sunny day and I was in the car with my dear partner Erisana looking out from the window into a beautiful natural landscape in Sao Paulo, Brazil, when I came up with the urge and inspiration of this story. While in the car, I started "downloading" the story from the beginning. A few hours later, I found myself in a busy mall, "Shopping Bourbon" in the heart of Sao Paulo and where I turned on my laptop and started typing out the first chapter as the ideas were still fresh in my mind. I, then, continued writing every day the story of Danny's quest to find his homeless uncle and. more than that, to find his real self. It wasn't that I was thinking what to write, it was as if there was something else thinking within me and telling me the story. Some people call it creative writing. Could it be my endless imagination? My rich memories in my unconscious? Could it be my higher self? Could it be that I was guided by the spirit realm, by a Higher Intelligence, a collective unconscious, by God? I can't answer these questions as I don't know what is happening when I intuit things, when I see signs, when I experience the synchronicities that guide me further in my life, I just open myself to that and expect more while being thankful to the Universe, Nature, to the Higher Intelligence or whatever else is out there giving me faith and hope to move on.

When I finished writing this book, I had another intuition which was to search google for the name of the place where Danny's uncle was "God's nest". A blog came up that had the following message that in a synchronistic way echoes my message for you all.

*Dimitrios Papalexis, MCC*

## The God's Nest

It's about the faithful truth. It's about the light somehow, the warm and friendly light of God. No matter if you believe it or not, the truth is out there you just need to open your eyes.

This is so true. The truth is out there. It has always been. All the answers we are looking for are out there, but you have to go within yourself first and get to know yourself in order to find these answers. This is the paradox of life. This is the big secret.

I send my blessings to you all. Wherever you are, I want you to know that you are my brothers and sisters, because as I once read: "Strangers are family that you have yet come to know".

# Questions for Reflection

1. Why wasn't Danny happy with his life? What was missing? What is missing from your life that would make you happier?

2. Do you think that Danny would have been better if he had stayed in Sydney and ignored his dream and hunch? Do you have any dreams or hunches telling you what you need to do?

3. Do you agree with Danny's decision to leave everything behind and go to New York? Do you have any personal experience of feeling, like doing something that you would have to risk a lot?

4. What do you think of Danny's best friend, John's, reaction of his news? How are your friends and people that you talk to daily support you on your decisions?

5. How did Rosa handle all this? What would you feel if you had to talk to your partner about something that would risk your relationship?

6. What do you think of Danny's father? How does your family react towards your decisions about life?

7. What happened in the aeroplane? Did you have any similar experiences of synchronicity and quantum moments/epiphanies?

8.  How did Danny make a difference in the taxi driver's life? How do you talk to people that you meet randomly in the streets? Do you really talk to them and listen to them? Is there real communication? Are you open to changing their lives and have your life changed by them?

9.  Why did Danny feel so good eating that soup in the pub? Is there any food or hot beverage that really helps you feel better in your life? Do you eat consciously?

10. Why do you think the homeless man didn't tell Danny about his uncle? When people are helpful with you and when are they not?

11. Why do you think the thieves hurt Danny? Was there anything positive in this situation?

12. What do you do when you get too stressed and you can't relax? Do you have any technique to deal with stressful situations?

13. What do you think of the temple? Is there any place or people you have met that had a significant impact in your life?

14. How did praying help Danny with his recovery and mission? What do you think of prayer? What role does it play in your life? Do you have to abide to a religion to pray? Do you feel comfortable hearing or saying the word God?

15. What did you understand about energy healing from the story? Did you have any experience of receiving energy healing? How is touching important in your life?

16. What do you think of Danny's homeless uncle? Why did he leave society? Do you agree with him? What can we learn from homeless people?

17. Do you think Danny will die after all? What is Karma for you? How can we change our Karma?

18. What do you think will happen to Danny if he goes back home? Do you think his life will change?

19. After reading this story, what will you change in your life? Is there a message or lesson from the story that can help you bring some positive change in your life?

20. Who are you?

21. What do you really want?

22. How are you going to get it?

23. What is your mission in life? What are your unique talents?

24. Are you afraid of death?

25. Do you believe in God? What is God for you? How would you feel if you were told that you are God like?

# About the Author

**Dimitrios Papalexis** is a personal development advocate, author, motivational speaker, Reiki master, and spiritual teacher with diverse experience from Greece, Australia and now Brazil. Dimitrios holds a bachelor degree in greek literature and applied linguistics from the Aristotle University of Thessaloniki in Greece and a master's degree in cross-culture communication from The University of Sydney in Australia. He has lived and worked in Greece, Australia, and now Brazil, where he is actively involved in a research about homeless people. He is also the founder of the project Instant Transformation, offering workshops for companies, schools and individuals. Dimitrios lives in Brazil with his partner, Erisana, their son Leonardo Constantinos and their dogs.